A LOVE FOR THE PAGES

JOY PENNY

I just stepped off the train this morning, and already by the afternoon I'm a soccer mom. Well, the 'game' is track and field, not soccer, and Mom sold the Caravan while I was gone and replaced it with this compact sedan, but it's basically the same thing. I'm sitting here in the car parked with four vans one way and three vans the other, just another woman here to pick up her kid. Okay, my brother isn't 'my kid,' either. I'm a track and field sister, not a soccer mom. The point is, I'm already counting the days until summer is over. Huh. Never thought I'd say that. At least I didn't before college, anyway.

I get a glance every few seconds through the space between two bleachers of one scrawny high schooler after the other stumbling across the track, his arms scrunched against his chest, his mouth open in probably stilted breaths. If pressed to admit it, such a sight used to excite me. Now they all seem like little boys. I unscrew the bottle cap on my lemon tea and take a swig with one hand, rifling through my purse with the other. I find what I'm looking for and slip the well-worn copy of *Pride and Prejudice* onto my lap. I open it one-handed to the page with the most recently bent corner, the book flopping open easily thanks to the wrinkles of the multiple creases peppering the spine. I take another drink, my gaze hitting the corner of my Kindle case sticking out of my purse on the passenger seat. A hundred e-books and counting, and one of my three beat-to-a-pulp favorites are almost always in my hand in those moments between doing something and doing something else. *"Now maybe you can get rid of the books taking up all that space in your room."* Mom beamed as she handed me the graduation gift—it was definitely thoughtful of her. Surprisingly thoughtful. Until Mr. Wonderful opened his mouth and revealed it was less about celebrating my interests and more about being practical, as usual. *"You can't bring a bookshelf to a dorm. You're going to share the space with someone new, and it's rude to bring a bunch of junk that'll just take up space."* Cooper always seemed to forget I was rooming with Deana. Still, he had a point. The books stayed behind mostly. Except for the three books practically starting to disintegrate.

There's a pounding at my window. I jump, sloshing the open tea bottle all over my lap—all over *my book.* I scream and am rewarded with muffled laughter. I slam the bottle into the cup holder and am ready to shoot Owen my most 'you're moronic' look and immediately feel my face flush as I come face-to-face with Sinjin through the driver's side window. I look away quickly, like staring at the steering wheel and ignoring the drops of tea on my lap will make the whole situation disappear. There's more laughter from the other side of the car and more pounding, too. I just keep staring ahead.

"Open up!"

I snap out of it, flicking the unlock button on my side and crossing my arms as Owen opens the back passenger door and tosses his filthy gym bag onto the back seat. I can't bring myself to look to see if Sinjin is still standing there, but even so, I feel this *presence,* like the shivers running down my spine are my own Spidey sense warning me, "He's here. He's here. Don't make a fool of yourself."

Too late for that.

"Yo, earth to Spoon! Guess you killed her, SJ." I hate when Owen calls him that. I hate when Owen calls me Spoon. No one else needs to turn every name on the planet into something new.

My own personal your-ex-boyfriend-okay-you-just-went-to-three-dances-together-and-never-officially-became-an-item-so-is-that-really-an-ex-boyfriend-is-nearby Spidey sense relaxes—and where exactly was that superpower before he pounded on the car window?—and I breathe a sigh of relief. I suddenly remember my wounded (paperback) warrior on my lap and scramble for the Kleenex box on the floor behind the seat, grabbing one tissue after another in painstaking single serve doses, and I look up just in time to see Sinjin bumping his fist against Owen's shoulder, laughing, smiling that chiseled Greek-god smile that lights up his gorgeous dark skin, and I freeze again.

"Hey, how's it going, June?" Sinjin runs a hand through his short black hair and speaks to me casually, as if we see each other regularly, even though we haven't seen each other for months—that little blip over Spring Break while hanging with Margot and Deana hardly counts. His tone gives no indication I'm a laughing stock for falling head over heels at first sight with my best friends' brother. My best friends' *younger* brother. My best friends' he-was-a-freshman-and-I-was-a-junior-the-first-time-I-saw-him-but-how-was-I-to-know-since-he-just-transferred-in younger brother.

I will my hand to finish pulling the fifth tissue out of the box and add it to the crumpled wad forming in my fist. "Great," I lie, mumbling.

Owen finds this hilarious. But Owen finds most things to do with me hilarious. I'm *so* glad to see the last few weeks haven't changed him. As if somehow when I felt like I'd aged a decade as I was cramming like mad for finals and writing half a dozen papers, the world would have also progressed a dozen years and I could look forward to finding a far more mature brother when I got home for more than the occasional weekend visit. No such luck.

Sinjin walks away, and I twist myself back into my seat and dab my book and lap with the tissues. *Okay, good. Bye. Take your Greek-*

god smile and your smooth, silky, gorgeous jet black hair to some other hapless victim.

The passenger door opens beside me. "I'm sorry about that." Sinjin pokes his head in. I cringe and do my best to smile. "I didn't mean to scare you. You just didn't notice us beside the car. Here, let me—" He scoops my purse up and lays it on the dashboard, climbing onto the seat. His fingers disappear around his side as he reaches into his pocket, pulling out a small washcloth.

I know what my Spidey sense should tell me. An athlete's hand towel. Probably used for mopping up sweat. About fifteen kinds of oh-my-god-gross. But Sinjin's hand is on my thigh, dabbing the tea stains as casually as if the liquid had spilled on the floor or on the seat. His palm lingers on my thigh—true, there's my pant leg and the washcloth between his skin and mine—but dear lord, his *hand* is on my *thigh* and I just about meld with the upholstery. He reaches his other hand out. "Let me."

I don't know what he wants—I almost hand him my wad of tissues—when he grabs the book from my hand. He raises his eyebrows. "You've got Kleenex on your book." He removes his hand and washcloth from my thigh and dabs at the book with it instead. "I'm so sorry." I don't bother telling him the book has already been soaked a time or two in the bathtub and there's no more damage that little tea spill could really have done to it. I just watch him at work, like a doctor and his patient, treating each wrinkled page with as much care as if it were made of silk.

"Wow." Owen slides into the back seat and shuts the door. "You're about thirty shades of red right now, June. What you're thinking is probably illegal in forty-eight states."

I don't bother asking where he came up with that number. I don't bother pointing out that at nineteen, there's probably some leniency for me to be fantasizing about a seventeen-year-old I used to sort of date. Instead I snort and grip the steering wheel, trying to fluff it off like the ribbing it's meant to be. "If you're guessing I'm thinking about murdering you right now for trying to embarrass me, I'd have to point out that's illegal in all fifty states."

The freeze in my spine lessens a bit as Sinjin shifts backward to exchange a look with Owen. They chuckle. "Finals didn't happen to give you a nervous breakdown, did they, June?" asks Sinjin.

"No, but seeing this place again almost did." I gesture at the bleachers and the two-story-brick-nightmare that is the high school I spent four years at far behind the field and the baseball diamond. I bite my lip as I look over. It's not so nightmare-inducing when I no longer have to spend my days there. At least back then, I didn't have to worry about so much. I didn't have to worry about practically anything. I smile awkwardly at Sinjin. "Thanks," I say reaching my hand out for the book. "That's, uh, good enough. It's nice seeing you."

"Oo, shot down, SJ. Shot down." Owen taps his palms against the back of the passenger seat. "But just as well. This whole sister-slash-best-friend thing has always kind of creeped me out."

I clear my throat. "There was no sister-slash-best-friend *thing*, Owen."

I can't help but notice Sinjin stiffen just a little out of the corner of my eye.

Owen reaches up to pat him on the shoulder. "College boys, SJ. No competing with them. Not when they're just a hallway away."

"There were no *college boys*," I hiss. I turn around to face him, not sure whether to throttle my little brother or just play it cool by not assaulting him despite the ever-present desire to do so. A lecture about how much *work* college actually is—well, for some of us anyway, those of us who just don't have time to date and mess around—is forming on my tongue when my purse starts shaking on the dashboard. I shut my mouth and hope my eyes are enough to convey the world of hurt Owen just escaped. I toss the book atop the dashboard and scramble for the purse, my hand resting on Sinjin's as he reaches at the same moment. We smile at one another like we'd just been caught doing something very wrong and I let go so he can pass me the purse.

"Thanks," I squeak, my voice hardly registering the calm and confidence I meant for it to. I fumble inside and pull out my phone to read the all-important text waiting there: WHR R U 2? DINNER and what's probably a frosty, shivering emoticon but looks more like a blue blob of water. It likely took Mom twice as long to compose that text as it did for her to make dinner.

"It's Mom," I say, shoving the phone back into the purse. I grab *Pride and Prejudice* and shove that inside, too, tea stains or no.

"Let me guess," says Owen. "She sent you to pick me up so she can make a 'Welcome home, June' dinner. And she timed it so we'd start eating about one second after my practice ended."

"Pretty much." I grimace and turn my head just slightly to give Sinjin a smile. "We should get going."

"Sure." Sinjin takes the hint and nods, sliding out the door. "Mamma probably has her own 'Welcome home, twins, make your own dinner' planned." I pinch my lips picturing Margot and Deana coming home to an empty house this afternoon. A gloriously relaxing empty house. Sinjin does this informal salute thing, like he's saying 'hats off to you.' "See ya!"

I grunt something back. Maybe it's the "see ya" I meant to say. Maybe it's some other language. My hands are kind of shaking on the steering wheel.

Owen shuts the door. "Well, are you going to start the car or should I drive?"

"Ha," I say, snapping out of it. I toss my purse back on the seat so recently vacated by the walking reminder of a simpler life, a life where I could have a little crush without feeling like some perv and without worrying I'm wasting my time even expending brain cells on anything but the future and work and research. I shake my head and start the engine, looking behind me to make sure there's no one I'm about to hit with my vehicle. "Mom told me you're not driving until you're forty-three."

Owen crosses his arms and leans back into the seat, squishing his damp blond curls against the headrest. "Mom's just being anal." He shrugs, closing his eyes. "Show me a junior in high school who hasn't snuck out in the middle of the night with his parents' car and a learner's permit, and I'll show you this little

horned horse I've been keeping under my bed called a unicorn."
He snorts. "That is, an actual human junior. Not Spoon from two
years ago, who wouldn't come up for air from a book."

Is it too late to get back on the train to Chicago? I'm sensing I
won't be able to make it through the summer without 'accidentally' hitting my brother with a vehicle.

CHAPTER TWO

"So two As and three Bs." Cooper states this fact as if he's the first one to give me the news, instead of echoing what I just said in answer to his question. He'd waited until Owen had wolfed down his fish, rice and veggies and excused himself from the table, tossing his plate and utensils into the dishwasher, eager to get upstairs to his world of Xbox and headset gaming. Since I eat at the rate of a normal human, I'm not so lucky to escape just yet. Cooper ponders the broccoli on his fork a minute, trying to divine my future from five final grades and steamed greens. "That's decent, Junie." He sticks his fortune-telling vegetable into his mouth. "Decent enough."

I take a deep breath and decide not to point out that I doubt very much he got straight As while studying to do something I don't even understand in sales for a plastic container company that has to do with 'business intelligence.' Because you'd have to be able to spell 'business intelligence' to pull off anything more than a C. I decide to put another forkful of fish into my mouth instead. Mom was right. It's cold.

"But those are just the finals, sweetie." Mom can't even choose a more adult nickname for her true love of six years. Every time she talks to him, I'm reminded of how she'd talk to Owen and me when we were in elementary school. "I'm sure when June gets her grades for the semester, they'll be even more impressive." Her tone is just so that I'm not sure if the faith she's putting in my term grades is more of a threat than a hope.

"We have those already," I say, putting down my fork. Better to get it over with now, so I don't have to draw out the disappointment. "The professors uploaded them online after they graded the finals. Three As, a B+ and a B-." I cringe, like I just admitted it was me who snuck home from college to take their car on a joy ride, not Owen.

At least their reaction is somewhat different than I imagine it was when they discovered Owen's attempt at auditioning for NASCAR. Mom nods and manages to twist the corner of her mouth up slightly. "Well, isn't that nice?" she says as if I'm six years old and she's commenting on a drawing I've shown her. "Good job, dear."

Cooper puts his fork down and his elbows on the table, folding his hands together. *Oh, lovely. Here it comes.* "Let me guess," he says, no preamble, no pat on the back. "The As are in your electives?"

I put my own fork down, suddenly craving salty ramen chicken noodles instead of cold broiled fish. "Pre-19th Century English Literature," I answer, taking just a little pleasure in the way I'm speaking a foreign language when it comes to Cooper. "English Composition. American Lit."

Cooper nods, leaning his lips against his steepled index fingers. "And didn't I say if you focused so much on your minor now, you wouldn't devote proper attention to the foundation courses in your major?"

Macroeconomics. Financial Accounting. I put my hands in my lap, focusing on how short I've cut my finger nails. "English Composition *is* required for a business administration major," I mutter, not untruthfully. I don't add, "Though it might not have been when you were in college, based on the way you compose an email."

"Oh, sweetie, let her be." I watch Mom push her chair back from the table, and she stacks her and Cooper's plates together, piling his fork and knife atop hers. "We both agreed it made sense for her to hurry up and get her minor done and over with, if she wanted. Then she'd have her junior and senior years to focus entirely on her major and her thesis."

Joy. Can't wait for that.

Cooper shrugs and leans back in his chair, not offering to help Mom clean up after him—as usual. "I just don't see why she's bothering with a minor at all. Or if she must, why not something related to the major, like marketing?"

Because I'm struggling just to hold onto that B- in Financial Accounting as is. I clear my throat. "English interests me." I don't know why I say it. We've had this conversation before. What starts us talking is always different, but we end each conversation much the same.

"Are you going to be a teacher then?" Cooper asks not as if it's a legitimate career option, but as if reminding me that I could wind up a—gasp, *teacher*—is enough to scare me straight.

"No," I say, shrugging. It wasn't really something I'd had in mind.

"What then? A librarian, in an age when people are more likely to read a text than read a book, and digital is leaving paper behind? A *writer*?" The last word leaves a sour taste in his mouth, and I watch him try to wring it off his tongue as he puckers his face. He puts a finger on the table. "College is an *investment*, Junie. You don't throw tens of thousands of dollars at something and aim to make next to nothing from your time there in return."

He has a point. Which I begrudgingly give him time and time again. Is he ever going to be satisfied that I'm following his prescribed secret-to-success? "It's just a minor," I say at last, pushing my chair back. I stack my utensils atop my plate in silence, staring at fish bones instead of my step-dad. Truth is, I don't know what I want to be. And even if I still have three years left to figure it all out, Cooper and Mom are never going to be happy with me admitting I have no clue how to get to that strange and foreign land called adulthood from where I'm sitting. College is a change from high school, sure, but I think being lectured to from a dinner table as I clean up my dishes is a clear reminder that life really hasn't changed that much just because I went to 'sleep away educational camp' an hour's train ride away.

"What's a minor but a waste of time and tuition?" says Cooper. I'm hoping it'll blow over, as it always does. I rinse my plate and utensils and drop them in the dishwasher, not even looking at Mom's face to see if she's listening. She hums and scoops two slices of chocolate cake onto plates without asking if I want some, which makes her lack of attention clear enough.

I turn to go and find Cooper standing, crossing his arms and looking down at me. He's at least a foot taller than me. Although most people are.

"I'll try harder next semester," I say at last, realizing there's no way I'm getting past him without some sort of under-duress promise.

"You better. That's *my* tuition money, too, you know." Cooper contributes to my college education. If I'm lucky, he won't launch into a rant about my sends-a-card-every-other-Christmas-without-a-return-address-so-Mom-can't-track-him-down-for-child-support father's lack of character for not doing the same. He reaches out and puts a hand on my shoulder, and I have to stop myself from flinching. "And I'm *investing* in you. Because I believe in you, Junie."

He means well, I suppose. It's how he shows he cares. Not by doing something like maybe noticing that no one else has called me Junie since I was thirteen, but it's something.

"Thanks," I say, and I do my best to smile.

He lets his hand fall and I have four seconds to pass before he launches into some other new lecture.

Not fast enough. "I hope you have plans for a job this

summer," I hear Cooper call from behind me before I can turn the corner and fly up the staircase. "Or an internship. Something productive." I'm about to cry, visions of a quiet, relaxing summer spent with my best friends on paper and my best friends in the flesh flittering away. "Because if not, I can always find you a temp position at work."

Dear god, I better find a job this summer.

<hr>

BEFORE I EVEN CONSIDER SHUTTING MY bedroom door behind me, I'm at my DVD tower and pulling out the DVD case my fingers land on. *2006, good enough.* I have to blow a thin coating of dust off of the Blu-ray player before I load up the title screen and plop down at the foot of my bed to watch. I'm only a few minutes into it, and Rochester is still just an anticipated memory, when the bed bounces and I just about scream bloody murder.

"Whatcha watching?" Owen asks, although I don't have to be a mind-reader to know he really doesn't care.

I jam my finger on the pause button and turn. Owen's picking up the *Jane Eyre* TV series DVD case I dropped on the bed behind me and holding it out as he glances between the case in his hand and the cases on the tower. "Just how many versions of this movie do you have?" he asks, his tone suddenly genuinely curious.

I snatch the case out from his hand, knowing full well the top shelf of the tower is filled from one edge to the other with various TV and film versions of the same novel. "Not enough," I lie, considering the only other versions out there to add to my collection might be theatrical recordings or the Bollywood interpretation I've been eyeing. "And it's a book, not a movie."

Owen nods as if he's humoring me. "It must be one hell of a book to comprehend, since a dozen versions aren't enough for you to wrap your head around it."

I growl and push the power button on the remote to shut off

the TV. "I *comprehend* it fine. Not everyone watches a movie instead of reading the book for a school assignment."

Owen shrugs. "Not everyone obsesses over books boring enough to *be* school assignments, either, so what's your point?"

I stand up and shut the Blu-ray player off manually, just so I can cross my arms and stare Owen down. When he's sitting, it's actually possible. "Do you need something from me?"

Owen stares intently at my comforter and picks at some of the threading. I notice for the first time that he's still wearing his track and field jersey. His sweaty, dirty jersey. Ugh. "Can't a brother spend some time with his sister freshly back from the big wide world?"

I sigh and sit back next to Owen. "Chicago is hardly 'the big wide world.'"

Owen grins and meets my eye. "But pretty much any college campus *is*."

I shake my head. "I don't know where you're getting these ideas about college life, Owen, but divide the underage drinking and endless sex by a thousand and multiply the studying and writing research papers and attending classes by five hundred thousand in your picture, and that's more like what I've had to deal with."

"Cute, Spoon, but math was never my strongest subject."

Good luck facing Cooper's thou-shalt-be-practical-when-applying-for-college speeches this fall then.

Owen gets up and walks over to the haphazardly stacked boxes I brought with me from Chicago earlier. He glances at the half-open tops like he's hoping to find some evidence of booze and condoms. "Sounds to me like there's plenty of fun to be had in college," he says. "You just chose not to participate in it."

I bite the inside of my cheek. "Do you have an inside source or something?"

Owen looks down the bridge of his nose. "Your own roommate made college seem plenty fun."

Of course. Though I can't picture Deana bothering to become

text buddies with my brother, I'm sure she told Sinjin a few things, who no doubt told Owen. Although why two nerdy older sisters who went off to college and stopped embarrassing their younger brothers at school should be a topic of conversation between the two, I can't figure. I let out a rather exaggerated breath of air. "Well, you'd know better than I would apparently. I hardly saw her after the first semester."

There. I'd said it aloud. The other reason why my first year of college was hell: one of my best friends became a stranger to me.

"Uh oh. Trouble in nerdy book lover paradise?" Owen might be genuinely concerned. He *seems* genuinely intrigued anyway as he plops onto the desk chair beside the boxes.

I bend my fingers inward, mulling over how dull my nails have gotten. "Deana didn't say anything about me to Sinjin?"

Owen snorts. "If she did, do you think he'd tell me?"

I drop my hand and grip the comforter. "He wouldn't?"

Owen rolls his eyes and leans back in the chair, his arms folded behind his head. "After the whole it's-awkward-you're-dating-my-sister thing we went through? No way."

"We weren't *dating*," I tell him for the millionth time. But I can feel the flush biting my cheeks.

Owen brings one arm down on the armrests and rolls one of his shoulders under his hand, cradling some apparent athletic soreness. "Well, whatever. Inviting you into our pre-Homecoming get-togethers when he couldn't bring himself to go to *your* people's and hang out with *his* sisters about proves my point."

"Hanging with underclassmen was awkward for me too." But that's old news. It doesn't mean anything anymore. I'm not going to see Sinjin much before it's back to Chicago and probably a new roommate, so it's over. And it *is* over. Even though I'd sort of hoped we could be friends again, I can't picture Deana wanting to hang this summer after ignoring me the first half of the year. Margot would be back from U of M, but somehow my other best friend had become some sort of online pen pal, a person you check in with every few weeks to share some edited version of your life.

"Studying hard for exams!" "Twelve inches of snow! It's going to be a pain walking to classes!" No "My classes suck ass." No "Your sister isn't who I thought she was, and the last time I talked to her she reminded me how pathetic it was that I could count the dates I've had on one hand since getting here—and I pointed out she doesn't have enough fingers and toes to count her one-night stands." No "Every day is a pain, and the only thing standing between me and jumping into that mountain of snow and never resurfacing is my imaginary book boyfriends and some crinkly almost-destroyed paperbacks."

I find myself picking at the open DVD case, like maybe the answers to everything are hidden in there.

Owen gets bored with my moping and stands. "I take it I can't ask you for a lift to SJ's for Deana and Margot's farewell party then?"

My fingers freeze on Rochester's scowl. "Their *what*?"

"Uh oh." Owen laughs, and there's more than just a little pity in his chuckle. "I take it Deana didn't tell you then?"

"She hasn't told me much of *anything*." I grit my teeth, hurling insults at her in my head. "What do you mean 'farewell'?"

"They're going on a European tour this summer." Owen cocks his head and crosses his arms. "I wondered why you didn't say anything to Mom and Cooper. But then I figured you might not want to figure out how to have the conversation with them about how wasting the summer in Europe could somehow prove beneficial to becoming Great Businessperson in the Family Mach II."

He has a point. I probably wouldn't have bothered to ask their blessing to go to Europe. I wouldn't have had the money to go either, really. But still. "I wasn't *invited*." I pinch my lips. "But it's a Ravi family thing?"

"Nope." Owen's grin is forced, and I can't help but notice his face is the perfect representation of 'sheepish.' "Just the twins. Maybe some friends, too."

Well, there's the rub, to quote the Bard. *Friends*. Friends actually talk to each other without arguing on occasion. Friends actually talk to each other period. Friends can rely on each other, can send more than the barest of "Yay, look at the surface of my not-at-all-this-happy life!" messages to one another.

And then my phone buzzes from the desk. Owen reaches across the boxes to grab it and hand it to me. "Can't be Mom," he jokes. "Unless she forgot you're upstairs."

I take the phone from him, although I have no idea who it could be. A last-minute invite to this apparently so-secret-Sinjin-sort-of-lied-to-cover-for-it party? My stomach flutters a moment when I see it's a text from Margot, complete with an emoticon clasping its hands together above its head:

Can I ask a HUGE favor?

Favors don't usually involve going to parties.

CHAPTER THREE

"**S**o you're cool with this? I knew you would be!" Margot doesn't even wait for my reply. Not that she doesn't already have it. But it's all she says to me this evening, posing the question and answering it herself every few minutes like she's run out of anything else to say. And she probably has. I know I have.

We spent the first ten minutes or so sharing awkward, stilted stories about how finals went and what else we'd been up to on our respective campuses since we'd last checked in with each other. Well, we were always 'checking in' with each other every few days on Facebook, Tumblr or Twitter. There were the photos she posted of her sorority banquet, the occasional famous figure quotes that *truly* moved her that morning, and the inside jokes tagged with her U of M friends and sisters. That about summed up all I needed to know apparently.

Between patting my thigh and smiling like a supermodel, she'd somehow glossed over how the European tour came about and whether or not anyone else was invited. But she certainly didn't skimp when it came to the favor she so desperately needed from me: "Do you have any plans this summer?"

I'd eyed the plastic cup she'd given me full of some sort of disgusting knockoff cola suspiciously when she'd asked. She certainly wasn't inviting me along with her and Deana—especially after I'd learned they were leaving *tomorrow*. "No," I'd said at last, truthfully. "Mom and Cooper want me to get a job, but I haven't even started applying."

Margot clapped her hands together like she found the news delightful. Glad someone did. "How about a volunteer experience instead?" She winked. "It'd look great on a resume!"

Somehow I wasn't sure Mom and Cooper would weigh the value of experience with the value of doing something that actually earns you money, but then again, I supposed it depended on the experience. Cooper had mentioned internships as being acceptable. I took a swig more out of the need for something to do than a genuine thirst for flat bubbly sugar water. "Doing what?"

"At the library!" Margot laughed. "I kind of promised I would help out all summer before the European plans became a thing." She cleared her throat. "I mean, it's a volunteer thing, but they're very strict about who's doing what for what hours. And I'd feel bad if I didn't have an equally qualified candidate to recommend to take my place."

I wasn't sure what qualified me other than a love of classic literature, and how that might translate to practical work experience. Still, staring at the liquid sloshing in my cup, I felt the tension in my muscles lighten just a bit. I had to do *something* this summer, and if I didn't find something to do fairly quick, that *something* was bound to be working at Cooper's office. And a *library*. "Sounds... cool." I responded. I wasn't at all sure how I'd pitch it to Mom and Cooper, but after the welcome home I'd already had, there might have been just the smallest rebellion boiling over inside me.

"Awesome!' Margot's lips became Van-Gogh's-perfect-smile-on-woman again. "Sinjin will be so glad you're the one to volunteer with him!"

Oh, shit.

Margot is just about done telling me she'll make the arrangements with 'Violet' tomorrow like I have any idea who Violet is even though she'll be *so insanely* busy last-minute packing and getting to the airport and catching her flight, and I have the feeling I'm supposed to be grateful she's going to make the arrangements. She suggests I report at '8 a.m. sharp' on Monday because *Violet* is a stickler for rules, and I suddenly have no idea how Margot knows the library staff so well she's even got an idea of their need for punctuality. I run through summer jobs my best friends have had in my head, and 'librarian volunteer' pops up as a rather minor blip in Margot and Deana's lives the summer before senior year—I specifically remember because they said they'd first fallen in love with the library during a brief summer they lived in the area while their dad consulted for a local company, years before they moved more permanently. They'd asked if I'd wanted to help out, and then before I even showed up, they told me the library had 'enough volunteers,' like too much free labor was ever a bad thing.

"We should chat," says Margot, even though we're already doing just that and failing miserably. "You've got an iPhone, too, right? When I'm in Europe, let's video chat so you can see the sights along with me!"

I know I'm probably smiling—what else can I do in a situation like this one?—but I don't feel very happy. "Sure," I say. Maybe she won't be calling so much once she bothers talking to Deana about me. I'm not sure why she doesn't know already.

"Margot! You're not going with us to Nice next month?!" A girl I don't know swoops in and sits on Margot's other side, her little mouth pinched and her eyes focused like this is serious business.

Margot doesn't introduce me and instead starts discussing her plans with the new friend, how she's spending an extra day in Paris with people I've never heard of, how she and Deana have got a homestay lined up while some of the group splits off to other parts of France and Italy. I hear just enough to wonder whether Margot and Deana are really going on their own vacation and just happen to be meeting up with others along the way or if she's off tomorrow with a large group that somehow breaks apart and disperses to various parts of the continent as the months pass. I don't feel much like asking.

I get up to toss the cup in the garbage and nibble on one of the stale pretzels in a bowl in the corner of the room. I rifle through my purse for the paperback and realize I shelved it when I grabbed the smaller purse from the back of my closet that I used to use for parties. And I didn't even pack my Kindle. Well, the light isn't exactly the brightest in this corner of the living room; Margot and Deana seem to have tried for some venue halfway between 'teen party without the pizza' and 'grown up wine and cheese noshing' and that entails a dimmer switch, the light barely emanating a glow. Still, I feel awkward with a pretzel and nothing else in my hand, in the corner while everyone else is chatting. I don't feel like looking for Owen and getting out of this place just yet because I know he's in the basement with Sinjin. I take my phone out of my pocket and pull up Google book search.

"He evidently wished no repetition of my intrusion," I read Lockwood say. Poor Lockwood, the most forgotten character in all of *Wuthering Heights*, despite the fact that about half the story is told from his narration. *"I shall go, notwithstanding. It is astonishing how sociable I feel myself compared with him."*

It's a sad evening indeed when I'm comparing myself to Heathcliff, but even invisible Lockwood would probably say the same of me.

"Important texts or something?"

I'm so lost in the well-tread world of the opening to the third story in my most cherished collection that I don't even notice Deana standing beside me until she speaks. She grabs a mouthful of pretzels and jams them between her teeth.

I clear my throat and stuff the phone awkwardly into my purse. "Or something," I say. It sounds bitchy even though I don't mean it to. At least I don't think I do.

Deana's eyebrow arches. "Well, it can't be research even now that school's let out, can it?"

"No," I answer, and I can tell I'm not going to be able to keep calm around her. "I don't have a strong desire to study macroeconomics now that I'm free of the subject for a few months, thank you very much."

"You could have fooled me." Deana laughs, but even I can tell she doesn't really find it funny. "At least you don't have your nose in an old, decrepit book for once." She crinkles her nose at the idea, although we used to stay up late during weekend sleepovers watching the very same stories together on DVD.

I say nothing. I adjust my purse strap farther up my shoulder and wonder how best to make my exit. Even if it might mean leaving my little brother behind.

"Margot tells me she got you to take over for her volunteer position with Sinjin." Deana grabs a handful of M&Ms and pops them into her mouth one at a time.

"Yeah," I say. If anyone's going to bring up the reason I've been asked, the little trip to Europe I've been unaware of until several hours earlier, it's not going to be me. "I start Monday."

Deana shakes her head. "Good luck." She speaks as if I'm really going to *need* it, and she's not all that sure I'm not going to fail.

"It's just a volunteer position," I mumble. I don't bother to add that if I fail to take it much more seriously than that, I'm probably not going to have luck justifying it to my parents.

"That's what I thought, too." Deana grabs a napkin and wipes her rainbow-colored palms together. "I used to *dream* of working in a library, you know?"

Yeah, back when we actually had something in common.

Deana tosses the crumpled napkin in a garbage bag set up beside the table. Really classy decorative touch, by the way. "But there's a reason why *I* didn't sign up to volunteer there this summer, even before Margot arranged the European homestay for us and her friends."

I try to pinch my lips together. I really do. "You mean besides the fact that you can't be bothered wasting time someplace you're not likely to get laid?" So much for subtlety. But she started it.

Deana's eyes widen a moment before her brows narrow. "Do you have a problem with me or something?"

She's not that much taller than me, but she may as well be six feet. Though she's not laying a hand on me, I feel myself being pushed more and more into the corner. I break eye contact first, clutching my purse strap with one hand like it'll give me support. "No more than you have with me."

I hear Deana tsk. "You know, I thought maybe after a summer off, you might be less of a judgmental bitch next semester. But whatever. I'm not rooming with you next fall."

I cross my arms and clutch them tightly to my chest. "That's *fine* with me. Have fun in *Europe*." Somehow saying the word with an extra coating of sarcasm, like the continent is some rubber tire museum her parents forced her to visit on a road trip, doesn't quite have the effect I intended.

Deana grins and pops one last pretzel in her mouth and chews on it with relish like she's imagining it's my hopes and dreams. "Yeah, I will. Have fun at *Rockford Private Library*." She turns and joins Margot and her friends on the couch, sliding in effortlessly and putting her arms around a girl and a guy's shoulders.

Huh. Well. Her 'burn' made absolutely no sense, so score one for me.

CHAPTER FOUR

What Deana said on Friday suddenly makes a lot more sense.

I could almost feel the unspoken questions Mom and Cooper wanted to ask me over the weekend, but somewhere, someone, some friend with more successful children or some mommy blog, probably told them to give their kids some space after making demands of them, and they're probably just counting down until one week on the dot has passed and they can sit me down for the "You failed to secure a job in the one measly week allotted, so you're reporting to Cooper's office in the morning" talk.

So at least despite the fact that I was up at 6:30 in the morning —at least that could be said of college, scheduling the day not to begin before late morning wasn't too much of a problem—I could take a little pleasure in seeing Cooper's and Mom's bleary-pre-coffee faces looking a little startled to see me waltz in for breakfast. I figured it best to tell them about the volunteer position when they had work to get to —no time for a long debate on whether or not I was wasting my day, no time yet for them to digest their disappointment.

"It's a huge favor for Margot," I told them. "She even arranged it while on her way to Europe this weekend."

"Europe?!" Mom repeated, like the news made her morning. "My. It's been ages." She cradled her coffee mug dreamily.

There was no asking why I wasn't heading there myself, naturally. Cooper had just about formulated some kind of response—something about how he understood filling in as a favor, but he hoped I'd find a replacement for myself—but I was already around the corner and up the stairs, ready for my day-starting shower. He was gone by the time I headed back downstairs, my straw-colored hair carefully tied back into a half ponytail with minimal frizz escapage.

"Aw, honey, you're not wearing *that*, are you?" Mom's parting words of wisdom. Well, before the discussion about me borrowing her car and her hitching a ride back with Cooper so long as I dropped her off first and picked Owen up later.

I stand at the library now, my eyes averted to the gray pants and cardigan my mother found so unappealing, the ones I dug out of the back of my closet in preparation for the day. Maybe what really turned her nose was the scuffed navy blue flats that still fit me from Homecoming freshman year. The one I went to stag because my dating pool probably wasn't out of diapers yet. (A slight exaggeration, of course. But everyone else was sure not to let me forget it, so what's one more reminder of my embarrassing taste in the younger man?)

Ms. Violet Fax is droning on and on about a small corner of the library outfitted with the very latest in media access ports. "Patrons can of course check out tablets for use anywhere in the library," she says, lifting the tablet attached to the nearest desk by some retractable-dog-leash-like cord, "but having these *built-in* to the various media stations takes up less of the staff's time and makes everything much more convenient for the patrons."

I'm picking up only one in three sentences the woman is telling me. My Spidey sense is absolutely out of control because I'm side by side with Sinjin, who looks possibly even more stunning in a collared shirt and khakis, his hair no longer damp with sweat but perfectly coiffed and slightly off-part. *I never did get to run my hands through that hair.* I bite the inside of my cheek, reminding myself that those days are long behind me.

Ms. Fax punctuates the end of her latest explanation of the *public* library's amenities with one sentence I've heard her utter over and over in the past forty minutes: "And of course, this too is allowed only by the most appreciated generosity of the Rockford family."

From what I can tell, the entire library is "allowed only by the most appreciated generosity of the Rockford family" to the point where I have to wonder if there's any government funding for the place at all. And then it clicks with me: the *Rockford Private Library*. Open to the public, but pretty much owned by one apparently glorious and generous family who seems to really, really like books. Or having Ms. Fax extol their virtues over and over to unsuspecting volunteers.

Ms. Fax clasps her hands together. "Now, Mr. Ravi, I know we've had the pleasure of your presence on the volunteer rosters in the past, so that about covers the new additions made in the past year with the most appreciated generosity of the Rockford family. You may report now to Ms. Pollo for further instructions." She smiles at me. "But Ms. Eyermann, as this is your first time here, I have a few more things to show you."

She leaves no time for responses, simply turning on her heel and retreating into an adjoining room, her head held high, her palms still clasped together in front of her chest. Sinjin's lips twitch into a slight smile at me as he passes. "Sorry!" he mouths.

Sorry for leaving me alone with Ms. Fax? But who doesn't want to know how the illustrious Rockfords are responsible for shitting every brick and spitting out all the mortar?

I notice through the glass walls Ms. Fax has stopped inside the room and turned, her hands still clapped together, her eyes meeting mine expectantly. Her lips are twisted into some semblance of a smile, but the effect is more scary than welcoming.

Still, it works. I nod at Sinjin and hurry after Ms. Fax, stepping inside one quiet room from another.

"This," says Ms. Fax, as if she didn't have to pause and wait for me to follow, "is the picture book section and the story time room." She gestures behind me at the entrance, and I turn, not finding anything at all to look at. Other than Sinjin many yards away at the information desk, speaking with Gracia, the 'Ms. Pollo' Ms. Fax introduced me to earlier who then insisted we call her by her first name. Like pretty much everyone who works at the library. Everyone except Ms. Fax, whom the others still seem to call 'Violet' behind her back anyway. Not that *I* would. I'm still a little too intimidated for that.

"These walls," continues Ms. Fax, snapping me back to attention, "help contain the noise of the children and make story time much less disruptive. They were made possible by the most appreciated generosity of—"

"—the Rockford family," I finish for her. And then I press my lips together. Wow. I've really got to keep my tongue in check.

Ms. Fax is silent for just a moment, but she soon picks up steam again. "Why, yes. Our library owes much to the generosity of the Rockford family. Our budget is very constrained, you see, and I have no idea how we'd be able to keep everyone on staff and accumulate new materials without their donations, let alone make such drastic changes."

She gestures around her to the story room walls. It's cute. We walk down several aisles of bins containing storybooks to the back of the room. There's a table and chairs in wrought iron—uh, not very safe for kids—in the corner, surrounded by smaller, more comfortable cushions in rose patterns on the ground. The art on the wall resembles the backyard of a country home—maybe even a castle—complete with painted ivy traveling over brick walls and trompe l'oeil representations of rose bushes and a meadow. I look closer. 'Meadow' isn't the right word. 'Moor.' Green land dotted with gray pools of water, little bogs fading into gray skies in the distance. An odd choice perhaps for a children's room, but the illusion of sitting on the back porch of the 'country castle' is appealing. I'd have imagined I was a princess at that age, ignoring the bogs and focusing on the roses. Now I feel like one of the women in my favorite novels.

"It's a very lovely room," I say at last, realizing Ms. Fax is observing me looking at my surroundings.

Ms. Fax pinches her lips together. "Do you have an interest in children, Ms. Eyermann?"

I pull my eyes from the wrought iron chair—not a very comfortable one even for an adult storyteller, it dawns on me—and turn to face Ms. Fax. I can't tell if she wants to know for professional reasons or is making some form of intrusive small talk. I settle for displaying my ignorance. "Pardon?"

"*Children,*" repeats Ms. Fax, gesturing around her and closing her palms together again.

"I, uh, sure, someday, maybe—" Can I get my life together first before I worry about that? And maybe find someone to parent *with*? I can feel my face flushing.

"I meant if you thought yourself qualified to lead children's activities here at the library."

"Oh!" My tongue trips over itself in its rush to brush over the misunderstanding. "Sure. Yes, of course." I snap up and straighten my shoulders. "I mean, I've babysat a few times." Ms. Fax's disappointment is wildly evident on her face. "I have a younger brother," I add, not sure at all why I'm so desperate to prove myself qualified for something I didn't even know I'd be asked to do. So far library volunteer work has consisted of volunteering to hear Ms. Fax extol the virtues of the Rockford family, and now I'm asked if I'd like to become a nanny for children. I don't know what I pictured. Shelving books. Directing patrons to them. Reading them.

Ms. Fax's expression brightens somewhat. "Oh, good. Then perhaps I'll recommend you for the children's activities."

Is it too late to admit my brother is only two years younger than me?

It's too late for anything. Ms. Fax has turned on her heel and made her way down the aisles of book bins and I let a small sigh escape my lips as I follow after her. She leads back to the information desk where I started, to Gracia, although I see no sign of Sinjin.

"Ms. Pollo," says Ms. Fax pompously. "I leave Ms. Eyermann here in your hands for the remainder of the morning."

Oh, thank goodness. The tour is finally over.

"There's more for you to see, Ms. Eyermann, if you truly hope to understand the scope of the library's services." *Okay, not over.* "But I'm afraid I have several tasks that must be done before lunch."

"Oh, don't worry about it," I choke out. "You've been most generous to show me around—" I feel like she's rubbing off on me already.

"We'll continue in the afternoon." Ms. Fax pinches her lips together and raises her chin ever so slightly. "There's the multimedia wing to be seen."

"Oh. Thank you." Just how big is this library? I haven't been here since I was a kid, long before any of these additions. Dad used to take Owen and me here, so I've kind of avoided it for a while. And I had a thing for owning my own books in more recent years, and then I got my Kindle. But I do *not* remember the library being this complicated, however big it may have been. It looks like if we're going to examine every juncture where the walls meet and talk about the generosity of the Rockford family at each location, this is going to take all year.

Ms. Fax nods and walks away to the administrative area, and I turn to Gracia. I can't stop my shoulders from slumping.

Gracia plops a stack of papers and envelopes up on the counter and grins. "How're you holding up on your first day of Violet?"

I smile awkwardly. I'm probably not friendly enough to rib on my colleagues just yet. "Oh. Fine, thank you."

Gracia nods knowingly. "Sure, sure." She points to the stack.

"Why don't you stuff envelopes with Sinjin? I sent him over to the study area. It's nice and quiet."

I grab the stack and thank her. I take a few steps toward where Ms. Fax went on and on about the Rockford family and their idea to add the study area with individual sound-proof rooms for groups to work on projects together and I pause. I see Sinjin at a table inside one through the glass window on the door. He's totally focused on folding paper, and I have this brief moment where I picture him folding origami, an *artiste* hard at work in his private studio. I shake my head to clear it and enter the study room two rooms over.

BY THE TIME I've followed Ms. Fax around the library five times over for a re-examination of every addition, I'm surprised to find that the woman hasn't yet found the *books* worth mentioning. But if I bring that to her attention, who knows how many days I'll be trapped on her endless tour? I'm tired, my legs ache, and despite being surrounded by fiction, I haven't been able to read since my brief lunch break. The one I took a little early so I wouldn't be caught in an awkward situation with Sinjin maybe asking if we should eat together—but that was wishful thinking. Or not wishful thinking. Sinjin got to leave early, too; even though he has a long weekend for teacher conferences or something, he still has track and field practice. Which reminds me. I have to pick up Owen later from track and field. And maybe pick up a diaper bag, too, while I'm at it, since I'm clearly now his second mother.

And tomorrow Sinjin shifts to evening hours and I'm bound not to see him. At least for a few weeks, when his school lets out. Then I wonder if he'll be back to a daytime shift with me. And I wonder if the fact that I think that might be a bad thing is just proof that I'm not as over him as I hoped I was.

But I am over him. I was. Until I saw him again. Oh, forget it. What's my life without all the uncertainty and conflict?

"June, before you go—" Gracia actually interrupts Ms. Fax's tour as we pass by the information desk. She's standing, sorting through the papers on her desk while cradling a phone under her ear. She doesn't even look up, and I have to wonder if she's on hold, or if she happens to be speaking to someone else with the rather archaic name of June.

She stops shuffling papers and holds up a key. "Want to collect the books from the drop-off box?"

My eyes dart immediately to the entryway and the dreadfully overcast skies. At lunch, the sun was still shining, but in the hours since I've been trapped in the Rockford Private Library and Museum, the skies have darkened so much that I wouldn't have been surprised if I'd gotten trapped in the library until long after the sun set without realizing.

Ms. Fax looks at me and then at the key dangling from Gracia's fingers. I jump when a flash of lightning darts across the sky, and the rumble of thunder echoes throughout the cavernous ceilings of the library mere seconds thereafter. Ms. Fax snatches the keys from Gracia—now back to her phone conversation—and hands them to me.

"Very well," she says. "We covered that this morning. I'll get you a bin."

I don't mention that Ms. Fax explicitly said it was the *pages* who typically went out to collect the books, as if the task were such an honor I'd have to work my way up to paid employee to do it. I glance awkwardly at the administrative desks, where everyone is inexplicably busy with computer screens and papers and books.

Thunder practically shakes the floor beneath my feet. That might explain the sudden promotion.

"Here you go," says Ms. Fax, holding out a plastic bin without a top. I take it from her and she glances toward the exit. "Work quickly. Be careful not to get the books wet."

As she returns to the administrative area, the sound of pouring raindrops assaulting the library roof tells me that's going to be impossible.

"Yes. Yes. 3 p.m." Gracia leans over the counter and drops an umbrella into my bin. She smiles, still talking to the person on the phone. "Every Wednesday."

At least she actually offered me a way to try to keep the books from soaking. I exhale deeply and trot past the security scanners and out the first set of doors to the entryway. It *would* rain on a day I thought it too warm to bother with my jacket.

I put the bin down near the outer doors beside a glass display case. As I futz around with the umbrella—Does standing between two sets of doors count as opening an umbrella while still indoors? How much worse can my luck get anyway?—I observe the open picture books and the fading cut-outs of apples and smiley faces in the display case. "Story time for children!" reads a yellowing banner that's drooping on one end. I have a feeling Cooper could tell them a thing or two about marketing. Or I should be able to. If I wasn't 'failing' with Bs in my business major courses.

The thunder isn't letting up, and I wonder for the briefest of moments if running outside just now with a metal umbrella rod and metal keys to a metal drop-off box is the safest thing to do, but I also consider that if I fail to do just that, I may not be welcome the next day. And Rockfords or no Rockfords, it beats being summoned to Cooper's office for the next three months. And at least I'll finally, for the first time since stepping into a library this morning, be touching books.

I balance the bin under the crook of my arm, swing open the umbrella and charge out into the misty early evening.

The box is just around the corner. Conveniently located for library patrons too lazy to get out of their cars to drop off books, but not so conveniently located for the volunteers sent out to deal with them. *I hope you're warm and dry and comfy in your car*, I think, to no one patron in particular. The wind is already assaulting my face from the side, sending an invisible powerhouse up and under the umbrella, careening it sideways so that I'm greeted with rain-drops to the face the instant I step out from beneath the overhang. I gasp, trying desperately to keep the umbrella from ripping out of my hands, skipping wildly against my will as the wind blows me along with the thing sideways.

I pass the box and toss the bin and keys onto the ground beside it so I can grab the umbrella with both hands. The rain is soaking through my cashmere sweater, forcing its way through my pants and soaking me through and through from socks to underwear. But I've gotten this far, damn it, and I'm not losing the one thing that has a chance of keeping the books from getting soaked, so I dig my worn-down-flat heels into the pavement.

Despite the roar of the rain and the whine of the wind, I hear a sort of clacking noise off in the distance. I can't see very well in front of me, and the umbrella isn't helping matters.

"Wait! Captain!"

I have no idea why someone is screaming about a captain, but then a great furry, wet mess is at my heels and I slam myself back against the drop-off box, the umbrella flying loose from my fingers.

It's a dog, and it's smarter than I am; it barely spares me a glance before running past and to the relative safety of the overhang.

There's a terrible jumble of noises from beside me after. The clinking I thought I heard comes to a sudden, screeching halt, just as a voice curses and the umbrella clangs against something. Or someone. There's a crash, and I see at once what was emerging from all the fog, a bicycle that's now skidding to the ground, crashing over its rider.

"Are you all right?" I ask at once, pushing aside the wet remains of my half ponytail as it whips across my eyes.

He doesn't reply, unless you count his non-stop string of swear words and chucking the bike aside.

"Can I help you?" I ask, crouching, watching as the grumpy wet creature brings his legs beneath him and tries to shift his weight onto his feet. He grimaces.

"Just. Just stand here." He points to an area beside him. I stand, not sure if he's asking me to shelter him a bit from the wind and rain.

Instead, he forces himself onto his knees, even despite the pain it so obviously causes him. The dog doesn't come to help, instead settling for barking its distress at its owner's fall from underneath the overhang.

"Captain! Quiet!" says the man, waving his hand angrily in the direction of the overhang, putting his weight now on one foot and hopping, tumbling over toward me.

I feel extraordinarily unhelpful. "Should I get someone from the library?"

He waves a hand. "No! I think it's just a sprain—argh!" He tumbles, almost losing his balance, leaning against the drop-off box for support.

I step beside him. "I really think I should get someone."

He hops. "No. No, but if you're so insistent, you might help me yourself." He reaches an arm out for support. "Please," he adds, more barking orders than pleading.

I slide in and wrap my hands around his back and chest to support him without thinking. I wanted to aim for his shoulders, but he, as everyone else in the world, stands quite a bit taller than I do. Instead, he wraps his own arm around my shoulders.

"I'm sorry about this," he says. "For… taking the liberty." His arm is heavy on my shoulder, and I have a feeling he might be sorry about leaning on a total stranger, but not *too* sorry considering she sort of maybe half caused his injury in the first place.

We start slowly back toward the overhang, the plastic bin soaked beyond redemption, the umbrella lost somewhere out there to the wild. It might be important to get the bike and bin out of the way, in case someone else drops off books, but I figure my first duty is to help him inside.

"And of course," he says, as if continuing a conversation, "it has to be *raining*. It wasn't raining when I set out."

"No," I say, loudly through the sheeting rain. "But it was on the forecast."

He snorts and takes a deep breath, pinching his lips together as his weight falls on the wounded ankle. "If you paid attention to such things yourself, would you have been out there, doing whatever it was you were doing?"

"It was raining when I went outside," I admit, steadying my feet as his weight pushes against me. "I wasn't supposed to be out long or get too wet."

"Ah," he says. "The umbrella." We're finally under the overhang, and the dog is lapping at our heels. "Move aside, Captain. And stay." The dog moves to an area beside the door and shakes itself out, sitting like a little proper dog gentleman, even if it's soaked to the bone. I'm surprised it so readily obeys its owner—when it's not being rained on, anyway. "You frightened me," says the man. "I wasn't expecting anyone out in this weather."

"Anyone but you, you mean?"

He laughs, but the sound is cut short by a grunt as he takes another step forward. "No one else stupid enough maybe." He tosses his head and a wet lock of dark hair falls over one eye. In spite of the overcast sky and the warm glow coming from the library providing just about the only light, I start to see his features. Despite the joking tone of his last comment, his dark eyes seem bothered, not fully in the moment. His thick brows are furrowed, his cheek bones sharp and angular, his nose perhaps just a tad too big. Still, he's almost handsome—the flush in his face, the raindrops masquerading a sweat on his skin certainly help—but not so much I feel uncomfortable about having my arms around his body. His lips pinch seductively—unintentionally, I assume—as he uses the weakened ankle. Well, not *too* uncomfortable anyway.

I peg him as mid-twenties maybe, but there's something about the way he carries himself, even with the ankle, that makes me think of him as older.

The first automatic door to the library opens and we stumble inside, dripping water all over the entryway floor. "You work here then?" asks the man. He keeps his eyes locked forward, his goal in sight.

"Yes. Well." I pause. "I volunteer. I just started today."

"Ah," says the man. "I'd nearly forgotten it was that time. Violet's fresh blood for the summer."

I tilt my head. I suppose someone who works part-time at the library might be coming just as my shift is ending, but why bring the dog to wait outside? It's not *that* warm yet. The second automatic door opens. Now we're dripping onto carpet.

Gracia lowers the phone from her ear at the information desk and gapes at us like we're… dripping water all over the precious made-possible-through-the-generosity-of-the-Rockfords carpet. Which I suppose we are.

"*Ms. Eyermann*, what on earth—" Ms. Fax appears from the administrative offices just as we cross through the security scanner. She puts a hand over her mouth. "You're hurt!" Her eyes are on the man leaning on me. I feel almost forgotten, but that's not a bad thing just at this moment.

"Wyatt! Bill!" Ms. Fax is actually shouting names—*given* names —of other workers toward the administrative area. I suppose I should have guessed from the tour that among the many things she values in the library, quiet is not one of them. "The first aid kit! Paper towels! Quickly!"

The few patrons sitting at couches and desks throughout the main area of the library put down their work to gawk as the two men come out to join Ms. Fax as she comes to meet us. I feel like part of an impromptu performance to advertize local theater.

Ms. Fax grabs a chair from a nearby table and scoots it closer to us. The man leaning on my shoulder shakes his head. "Please, Violet. No need to overreact. It's just a sprain, I think." He lets his hand fall from my shoulder and I loosen my grip, guiding him into the chair on one side as Ms. Fax supports him on the other. He looks from me to her and back. "I feel ridiculous."

Wyatt appears and swoops in with a roll of paper towels, tearing multiple sheets in just a few seconds and shoving them at the man. He takes them, regarding the crumpled-up soaking paper with a little disdain, and wipes his face. Wyatt is on the ground, spreading paper towel over the areas where the carpet has dampened.

"Never mind that!" says Ms. Fax, tapping her foot. "The first aid kit!"

"Right here, Ms. Fax." Bill trots out from behind the check-out desk.

Ms. Fax is shoving a chair in front of her injured patient, stooping down to lift his uninjured leg and place it on the chair.

The man stops her, grimacing as he bends to put his hands atop hers. "It's this one," he says. "And I don't need to ruin another of your chairs by getting it wet."

"You need to elevate it," says Ms. Fax. She turns to Bill. "Fetch an ice pack!" Bill hands her the first aid kit and leaves. Wyatt is still standing there, his paper towel roll in hand, not sure what to do.

The injured man grunts and pulls his leg back. "Violet, please. We're causing a scene." His gaze drifts behind her.

Ms. Fax turns around to see the curious library patrons staring, and she puts her finger to her lips, hushing the silent watchers with a "Shh!" It succeeds in getting a few to feign interest in their books and work again at least, even if she's directing the command in the wrong direction.

Ms. Fax's eyes fall first on Wyatt, then on me. "Make yourself useful, Mr. Temple! Ms. Eyermann!" Wyatt is immediately ripping paper towels off of the roll and tossing them on the floor. I watch, frozen. Ms. Fax's mouth puckers. "Where are the books and the bin?!"

I jump. "I didn't—He fell and—"

"Violet, please. It's pouring out there." The man is dabbing himself with his soggy paper towels, which are crumbling to bits in his fists. He laughs when he notices the pieces stuck to his black v-neck t-shirt. The shirt's either too tight or too wet or both—but I swear I can practically see through to the muscles beneath. And though he's not bulky in that you-work-out-way-too-much way, there are *definitely* muscles beneath.

"Yes, of course. Very well." Ms. Fax sighs and reaches a hand out toward me. "You may go. Return the key and we'll clean up your mess."

I feel horribly in the spotlight as Ms. Fax eyes me, and even Wyatt looks up from stomping paper towels into the ground and I catch the man who's injured watching me casually out of the corner of his eyes, pretending his focus is on drying himself with his meager towels. I pat my pants pockets and come up with nothing. "I left them outside—"

Ms. Fax's eyes widen in horror. "'Outside'?! *Outside?* Ms. Eyermann, those keys are for library and support staff *only*—"

"I'll go get them!" I say, turning on my heel before I have to listen to any more of her lecture. I see Bill running out from the administrative area just as I pass through the security gate and the first set of automatic doors. I'm out the second before I can make sense of any more of Ms. Fax's shrieking.

Captain the dog whimpers as I pass by, and I pat his head. He hasn't moved since taking up his position at the side of the door. I glance out at the sheet of rain piercing the muggy, foggy air. "Well, here goes nothing," I say, hoping the dog will at least fetch help if I don't make it back in one piece.

To say it's a battle with the wind and the rain is an understatement, but I manage, every second feeling like hours. I grab the plastic bin and feel a rush of relief to see the keys inside, floating in the pool of water accumulating. I run over and slide it under the overhang, feeling some sense of responsibility for moving the man's bike out of the way of any patrons' vehicles. I grab it and search vainly for the umbrella, but I'm afraid it's long gone. I make a mental note to show up the next morning with a brand new one for Gracia and try to push the bike along, but it freezes. The chain dangles and drags across the pavement. Perhaps it wasn't just the umbrella in the face that caused him to tumble.

Even though the bike is easily almost my match in height, or at least length, I lift it and feel my arm straining. I take one step after another into the blasting wind and finally, *finally* feel the brief break of being beneath the overhang. I lean the bike against the wall beside Captain, who watches curiously without so much as a noise. I half collapse against the wall beside him, catching my breath.

I'm cold. I'm tired. And I'm soaking, soaking wet. I glance down at my cardigan and pull it and my blouse out a bit away from my skin, feeling the fabric stretching and pulling down on me. I sigh and walk a few steps to snatch the plastic bin. I fish out the keys and turn the bin over, letting the water spill, not caring that it's splashing over my scuffed-up flats. I take the dripping, empty bin and keys back inside, passing through the first set of doors and nearly slamming into the dripping, injured man I'd helped inside as I pass through the second set.

Our eyes meet. He's leaning on one foot, and he's about to fall over. The very corner of his mouth twitches in what might be a smile. Or what might be a flash of annoyance. "Just checking on Captain," he says, and my hopes for at least being recognized for my heroic bike rescue are dashed.

"Mr. Rockford!" says Ms. Fax, flitting past the security gate from the administrative area. She slides in beside him to support him. "Please. You need to rest." She directs him back into the library, but not before looking me over from head to toe. "Thank you, Ms. Eyermann. Leave the library property here. No sense in you wetting the carpets any further."

I drop the bin and keys inside it just outside the security gate. *Mr. Rockford* continues to drip onto the carpet as he's directed back into his chair, Ms. Fax immediately positioning an ice pack from the floor over his ankle. Half her business suit is drenched from letting him lean against her.

I sigh and turn to go.

"See you tomorrow, June!"

I look back. Gracia is bending over the gate to grab the bin and keys from where I left them. She rolls her eyes and kind of tilts her head toward the scene behind her. She's holding out my purse.

That might help if I want to actually get going.

"Thanks," I mumble. "And sorry about the umbrella, it—"

Gracia shakes her head. "Don't worry about it."

I try to smile and wave my sopping, cold hand at her.

My phone buzzes as I step through the first set of automatic doors and I fish through my purse, leaving wet hand stains everywhere.

8 Missed Texts: WHR R U UR BRO PRACTICE CANCLD. PICK HIM UP!!!

Wet, cold, unappreciated *and* late. I shove the phone back into the purse and head out into the torrent.

CHAPTER FIVE

The rest of the week at the Rockford Private Library isn't nearly so eventful, but at least I stay dry. After a day or two of receiving a bit of the cold shoulder from Ms. Fax after the first day's debacle—she seems to think I might *dislike* a bit of peace and quiet in the library—things start to go rather smoothly. I only see Sinjin once, just from afar, as I end my shift. I'm left to complete volunteer tasks in relative peace, which means I'm free to listen to audiobook versions of my favorites while my hands do the labor.

Which leads my mind to embark on rather interesting flights of fancy that stick with me even on the weekend, when I'm at last free to relax in my room, leaning on pillows propped up against my headboard and letting the TV show me some image of vapid people arguing in clearly scripted fights about who promised what and when and where.

I'm lost in thought when my phone rings. It's the promised-but-not-at-all-expected first video chat from Margot.

I feel generous. I shut the TV off and answer. "Margot, hi!" I say. Margot looks like she's on the set for a romance movie set in Paris, some balcony in the dark with cutesy Old World buildings in the background. The phone must be leaning up on a table, as she's sitting there, her hands folded.

"*Bon soir*, June!" Margot waves. I'm suddenly conscious of wearing sweats and a headband; Margot's got on a cute scarf and blouse that make her look right at home as the Paris movie lead. She blows a kiss at the screen. "How've you been?"

"All right," I say, considering the number of utterly disastrous days I've had for the week has only totaled one. "How's France?"

"*Amazing!*" Margot's attention is suddenly focused off camera and she holds up two fingers. "*Deux, s'il vous plait. Oui. Oui.*" She turns back to me. "Sorry. Sorry for not calling earlier, but every day has been crazy."

I force a smile. "Sounds like it."

Margot points off screen. "Oh, that's just my host mom for the next month or so. She's *so cute*. Remember when Madame Reed told us the French have endless courses when it comes to dinners? Well, my *maman* here just won't stop feeding me. She's making me and Deana *chocolats* from scratch as we speak."

I chuckle. I want to make some crack about not gaining too much weight when abroad but it just seems forced and dumb and hurtful.

"So how's the library work going? You met Violet, of course, I take it?"

I shake my head and sigh. "Yeah. *Oh*, yeah, I met Ms. Fax. She gave me the full tour."

"That's right. *Ms. Fax.*" Margot laughs. An arm appears in the video holding a plate with what looks like two chocolate-covered berries. I'm drooling from across the globe. "*Merci.*"

A dark-haired woman bends around to pop on screen. "*Bon soir*, Jenna!"

"*Ce n'est pas Jenna, Maman.*" 'This isn't Jenna,' Margot's saying.

The woman squints her eyes as if she can somehow look harder and see me better. "*Bon soir, nouvelle amie americaine!*" She calls me a 'new American friend.' Like Margot's been calling a bunch of friends she's already 'met' by phone all week. Probably a Jenna more than once at that.

I wave at her with as much enthusiasm as I can muster. *"Bon soir!"* I say back. But she's already gone, and Margot is popping the first of the berries in her mouth, making such a ridiculous orgasmic noise I'm glad the volume on the phone isn't too loud.

"So good," says Margot, and she eats the second one.

I just sit there on my bed awkwardly watching her until she finally licks her fingers and sets down the plate. *"Anyway,* sorry about that." She folds her hands on the table again. "Any Ms. Fax horror stories?"

"Nothing I'm sure you haven't dealt with yourself," I say. I pick at the comforter with one hand, not quite comfortable looking Margot in the face. "Well, the first day was pretty insane. I almost thought I was going to get fired. Well, asked not to come back or whatever."

"What? Sinjin didn't mention *that.*"

"It was after he left for the day." I pause and examine the screen. Margot seems to be all ears, leaning toward her phone with wide eyes. "It was pouring out, and they sent me out to collect the books in the drop-off bin."

"On your first day?"

"It was raining." I chew on the inside of my cheek and wonder if I should bother telling her. Even if it really doesn't mean anything, I know she'll tease me. It's been ages since we've talked about boys. It's been ages since we've talked about anything. "I kind of threw an umbrella in a guy's face and caused him to fall off his bike and sprain his ankle. And that guy was one of Ms. Fax's 'most generous Rockfords.'"

I can hear Margot actually gasp. Points for the microphone power on this technology. "You *didn't.* Why on earth—?"

"Well, I didn't *throw* an umbrella exactly." I grin. "The wind tore it from my hands, and I really didn't see him coming."

Margot shakes her head, but she's beaming. "That must have

been something. I'm surprised you didn't give Ms. Fax a conniption."

"I just might have." I'm trying to smile, but my lips are trembling. "If I didn't *have to* do something this summer, I might not have had the courage to show up the next day."

If Margot noticed my little alluding to Cooper and Mom's summer work experience mandate, she doesn't say anything. Instead she's looking off screen, nodding her head slightly. "A male Rockford… I think her husband died years ago, so—Was he good looking?"

I'm back looking into Margot's eyes and she's clearly dying for more information. I bite my cheek and think. "He wasn't *bad* looking exactly." The image of that wet, tight, clinging shirt suddenly pops into my mind.

"You're blushing, oh my god!" Margot actually points at me through the camera.

"I am *not*," I say, shaking my head. "No, if anything, well… This is going to sound really stupid."

Margot folds her hands again and raises an eyebrow. "Go on."

"It's just—" Damn, trying to say what's been going through my mind out loud makes it sound really, really stupid. "I've been thinking about Mr. Rochester and how Jane first met him when she startled his horse and sent him toppling over. Rochester injured his ankle, too."

Margot does that snort-laugh thing she does, one I haven't heard in ages. Unless you count when she was laughing with other people at the going away party. "Jane *Eyre*? Oh my god, June, that is really crazy."

"I know." I shrug. "I don't really mean anything by it. I'm just passing the time."

"Sure." Margot winks exaggeratedly. "Passing the time by fantasizing that Everett Rockford is destined to be your own Mr. Rochester."

"Everett?" I wonder, briefly, if Margot's met my sopping wet man before, and suddenly the whole ridiculous thing seems incredibly more ridiculous. And less *mine* somehow.

Margot raises her shoulders slightly. "I assume that's who you met. No other man left in the Rockford family."

"You've met them all?"

Margot shrugs while regarding me curiously. "What's this, June? Are you prospecting your Mr. Rochester?"

"No. No." I try my best to seem casual, but I'm worried she'll notice a flush in my cheeks again. "I mean, would him reminding me of Mr. Rochester mean I find him attractive?"

"What, you aren't worried about an insane secret wife in his attic?" Margot flexes her hands and lengthens her arms, stretching. "Normally, I'd say no. But you don't think I remember all the books and movies and miniseries you got me into? I wasn't your best friend for half your high school experience without noticing your strange attraction to fictional jerks."

"*Fictional*," I reiterate.

Margot pinches her lips. "I'll grant you that. Well, maybe this is a good thing. You *not really* being into Mr. Rockford."

"Why?"

"Oh, *nothing*." Margot speaks the last word with far too much emphasis. I've a feeling she's luring me into a trap, but I don't feel like dealing with her teasing in order to divulge the truth out of her.

There's a knock and I hear Mom through the closed bedroom door. "June, can we get going? I want to be back in time to make dinner."

My eyes dart to the clock on my bed stand. A full hour before we'd agreed to leave. "Just a minute, Mom!" I scramble off the bed, taking the phone with me.

"What's going on?" I hear Margot ask. "Do you have to go?"

"Yeah, I guess." I lean the phone on a book stand on my desk and wave to her. "Sorry. Mom's insisting she take me, and I quote, 'proper business attire shopping.'"

Margot laughs. "What, the sweat suit and headband not flying at the library?"

"Ha ha." I find I'm actually smiling for once. This feels good. It feels like a few years ago.

"I'll let you go then. I'll call you soon!" Margot reaches a hand out toward her phone, and just before the feed cuts out, I hear, "Are you *still* talking to that snobby bi—"

Deana. Because things were going just a little too well.

<hr>

"Isn't this cute? I mean, the color is perfect for you!" Mom's holding a gray blazer in front of my torso and the sleeves extend about five inches past where my wrists end. She frowns. "Hmm. Maybe you need something tailored."

We've been in the women's department of some fancy clothing store at the mall I've never set foot in in my life for what must be three hours now. Mom's got a whole stack of suits, blouses and trousers she's come across for herself. Well, usually things she thinks will suit me, then they wind up resembling oversized clown suits when she dangles them in front of me. No sense in wasting the find, though, so into the 'for Mom' pile it goes.

"Mom, my clothes are fine." I did actually dress up a little before we left for the mall. Well, I'm wearing sneakers, but khakis and a light sweater over a tank is certainly a step up from the sweats I left at home.

Mom ignores me and picks another suit coat off of a rack. "Appearances make a big difference in the business world, June."

"It's just a library."

That's the wrong thing to say. Mom's lips are puckered, and I know if I walk out of here with nothing to show for her efforts, I'll not only hurt her feelings, I'll have provided one more piece of evidence on a platter that what I've been doing for the past week hardly qualifies as something worthwhile. My eyes dart to the ground and the sneakers. "I could definitely use some new dress shoes," I say, thinking of the scuffed up pair I ruined even further in the rain disaster.

"Of course, dear." Mom turns her attention back to the suit, which she holds out in front of her, examining every fiber for some secret that's lost to me. "In the back," she says, nodding her head in that direction.

I do my best to keep from exhaling the epic sigh of relief that's been building until I'm out of earshot. I make my way to the very back corner, telling not one, not two, but *three* store employees that I'm just looking, thank you, and making a break for the shelves of shoes I see calling me from the back corner by cutting through the men's section. I shimmy past a stand with a dress-shirt-and-tie torso, sending jealousy vibes to Owen for not having to stand *here* and watch as Mom dangles shirt after coat after tie in front of him, when I come around a display of handkerchiefs and smack right into a man's torso. An actual man's torso.

On instinct, I gaze up to face the man who's nearly pummeled me, and I can *feel* my face go several shades darker. He's very tall and very blond and very handsome with square-rimmed glasses. "Sorry," I say, averting my eyes past the man's white dress shirt and black pants to the floor and the man's shiny black dress shoes.

"No, I'm sorry. Are you all right?"

Seriously? I can't smack into a handsome guy who can just mumble 'sorry' and move on? No, I get stuck with the rare species of damn-good-looking gentleman.

"Yes, thanks." I back up and flatten myself against the display of handkerchiefs, wincing at the sound of the plastic crumpling behind me.

"Whoa!" The man dives, catching some of the packages to keep them from falling to the ground.

I feel, as if that were even possible, like I'm about to sink into the floor.

"Blake, what the devil are you up to? Hoping for a new career in product shelving?"

Okay, floor. You may as well open up and swallow me whole.

Behind the handsome blond juggling the apparently several dozen packages of handkerchiefs I've bumped into is the dark-haired man whose ankle I sprained in the rain—and he's clearly favoring his uninjured ankle now even as he stands there. He's dry now, his hair is wavier and arranged atop his head with more volume, somehow both messy and perfectly styled all at once. He's dressed in a black collared shirt this time, and the tightness wasn't just from the wetness during the rain—it's probably a size too small for him. His chest isn't as clear as it was when soaking, but I can still make out more than a few creases and bulges.

My eyes dart immediately to the ground, where I scramble to pick up the remaining packages 'Blake' wasn't able to catch for me. "I'm so sorry," I say, willing them both to go far, far away.

"Don't worry about it." Blake begins hanging his stack of packages back on the pegs, and I rush to follow suit, jamming a few more near the bottom.

"Oh, for heaven's sake, Blake. Let me call someone over."

"No!" I shout, looking up. Both men are staring at me. Blake is even frozen mid-package-hanging. I stand and reach out for the rest of Blake's packages. "No, I mean, let me. I knocked them over."

Blake doesn't hand me the few packages left so I snatch them rather forwardly from his hands and feel even more ridiculous as I slide the holes through the pegs as quickly as if my life depends on it.

"I should have known." Mr. Rockford—Everett?—neither feels right. *Rockford* takes a few steps closer. I can feel him examining me as I finally shove the last of the packages back into place. Well, as close to in place as I can be bothered to put them, seeing as how I'm dying to dart around the corner, run out the store, and pretend this never happened. "It's you, isn't it?" he asks, like I could possibly not be me and confirm my non-existence.

I fold an arm across my chest and squeeze my bicep. "Hi," I say, in no earthly tone. "Nice to—How's the ankle?"

Blake straightens up and regards Rockford from head to toe, lingering on his feet. "Just why *are* you limping, Ev?"

Rockford's lips pinch into a thin line and he catches my eye. "A bike accident," he says, without averting his gaze.

Blake nods. "Ah, that explains it." He looks back and forth between us. "So you two know each other?"

I'm about to explain our meeting at the library earlier in the week—maybe skimming over the whole umbrella-in-the-face part—when Rockford looks away, his attention drawn elsewhere. "Not at all. Blake, are we or are we not on a bit of a schedule? I suggest you find what we came for so we can go."

He retreats the other way, and Blake is left to watch him leave and then regard me curiously. "Sorry about that," he says. He nods and starts walking backward. "Nice meeting you!"

I'm left with my mouth agape wondering if that really counted as a proper introduction.

"Miss, may I help you?" One of the salespeople appears and examines the hastily hung collection of handkerchiefs wearily out of the corner of his eye.

"Ah, no." I point to the corner where I was headed. "Thank you. Just looking at shoes." I briskly walk over there before I'm asked any more questions.

I can't explain the oppressive feeling of crabbiness that takes over me. I just know that as I walk the racks of shoes in the shaded, lonely corner of the store, all I feel is a rising urge to run home screaming or to kick someone. Or both.

I take a deep breath and grab a few pairs of flats. At least with Mom still over by the suits, I won't have to explain why walking around balancing on uncomfortable high heels isn't appealing to me, even if I could use the extra boost in height. I bring my boxes to the very end of the aisle, where there's a bench for trying on shoes and some of those little sheer socks in a box. And, thank god, no one in sight. I need time to decompress and thwart my bloodlust.

I'm alone in the peace and quiet for a full five minutes—I've tried on all the shoes and even picked a pair, I'm just rifling through my purse for my paperback—when I hear footsteps approaching.

"All right, all right. I think you've had your fun already. Lay off, will you?"

"I'm just wondering why you didn't bother to tell me about the bike mishap. No, you'd rather limp and be all mysterious, let me think you wrestled a bear or something over the weekend and lost."

I release the grip on my book and turn my head slowly, willing to the gods of coincidence and accidents that there's someone else shopping in this store who's had a recent bike mishap. Someone else who speaks each word as if it's a terrible burden he's being generous to utter.

"And you want to tell me exactly who that woman was? The one you claimed not to know despite clearly saying 'it's you'?"

Through the space between shelves and the even smaller space between boxes, I see the torsos of two men. One's wearing black, the other white, just like Rockford and Blake. But I know that already. I try to breathe as quietly as possible, praying they'll quickly find what they're looking for, or at the very least go try them on at the other end of the aisles.

"I don't actually know her name," spits Rockford. I can hear someone picking up shoes every few seconds and letting them fall back into their boxes.

"But you've met her before."

Rockford exhales sharply. "On my way to the pavement on that horribly rainy day last week, yes."

"And she helped you up?"

"She *caused* me to fall."

I find I'm holding one of the shoes in my hand and have to stop myself from throwing it in his direction.

Blake laughs. "Oh. Well. I can see why you're so grumpy. Checking out a pretty girl and you fall flat on your face."

My fingers loosen their grip on the shoe. My face is suddenly burning. But not in a bad way.

"I think you need your eyes re-examined."

My breath catches in my throat.

"Ouch. That's harsh. She is *too* pretty, Rockford. Maybe you need *your* eyes examined."

I can hear someone, Rockford probably, smack his lips together. "She's bearable. Certainly nothing I'd, as you put it, 'check out.'" Bearable. *Bearable*?! "And I hardly think you're the best judge on the subject."

"Just because I'm gay doesn't mean I can't tell when a woman is attractive."

Talk about a double whammy. The handsome gentleman who complimented me without even knowing I was there to hear it isn't even into women. And the jackass jerk who is so focused on the fact that my umbrella flew into his face—and *by the way*, I wasn't the one biking in pouring rain, he might have run into me if I hadn't stopped him—not only doesn't appreciate that I helped him or saved his bike, he finds me *bearable*.

Good thing I don't give a rat's ass what that jerk thinks of me.

Rockford snorts. "Blake, can we agree to stop talking about it? I think I've devoted enough of my time to discussing a woman who shops by herself on a Saturday."

I'm not sure if that means he assumes I have no boyfriend or if that somehow makes some insulting sense in Bizarro man's head. Whatever the case, I'm on my feet, about ready to chuck the shoe down the aisle and pray I don't hit the poor nice gentleman who has the bad luck to be friends with that asshole.

"Honey, there you are! Come on, I'm ready to check out. Did you find anything?" Mom takes me by surprise coming up the aisle next to the one where Blake and Rockford are having their heated conversation about me, and the shoe slips entirely from my hand. That horrible mixture of wanting to thrash about the store knocking over all of the displays and wishing I could disappear into its walls washes over me and I just stand there, shell-shocked.

"June?" Mom asks, waving a hand in front of my face. About the last thing I need is for her to say my name. Not that he *knows* my name, but if I'm going to continue volunteering at the *Rockford Private Library* ...

"Yes," I mumble, bending down to pick up a box. I realize it's not the one I'd settled on, but at that point, I don't even care.

"Cute," says Mom, regarding the pair of brown loafers. "All right, let's go." She walks around me and heads down the aisle where Blake and Rockford are waiting.

"Wait!" I say, although I have no idea how I'll explain why I want her to wait. And regardless it's too late.

"Hmm?" Mom turns around.

"Nothing." I take a deep breath and follow her, my head held high. What do I care what they—

They're gone. I exhale and feel a rush of soothing calm wash over me. I straighten my shoulders and brush past Mom, the box of shoes cradled under my arm.

Bearable. Bearable. And suddenly the word 'tolerable' floats in my mind like a crazy reminder of the jerks I love.

CHAPTER SIX

o, I haven't seen "Mr. Rochester" at the library since. But I did run into him at the mall, and I have to tell you, I couldn't stop thinking about how similar the meeting was to when Eliza-beth Bennet first meets Mr. Darcy. And overhears him telling his friend she's "tolerable" and "not handsome enough to tempt" him.

After my second uneventful week at the library, I'm starting to get into the groove of what's expected of me. Lunch breaks are even tolerable knowing Sinjin isn't yet around during the day to have that awkward should-I-eat-with-him-because-it's-all-cool-but-it's-really-not debate with myself. Of course, Owen and Sinjin are done with school next week. And that probably means I'll be back to volunteering the same hours as Sinjin.

Remarkably, Margot answers my reply to her email—I don't know if that means we'll skip the video chat this week, but I suppose I should be thankful I'm remembered—all the way from France within minutes.

Okay, reality check, girl. First he's Mr. Rochester, now he's Mr. Darcy? In either case, you're either destined to come to love him despite his dickishness or you're dealing with the type of jerk who has no place in the 21st century. Either way, I'd advise you to run.

That's the only part of the email she actually replies to. But that feels right. It's the only part of the email I wrote without any of that 'how are you, I'm fine, here's the news about the edited, most pleasant façade of my life.'

I'm not sure what to say—and my lunch break is ending, anyway. I log out, close the browser down and stand up—coming face to face with Ms. Fax.

"Ms. Eyermann. I wonder if you might come with me to my office?" She tries to speak quietly because we're on the library floor, but there's no mistaking the edge in her tone.

"Of course," I say. Things were going too well anyway.

I follow Ms. Fax past Gracia at the information desk and Bill and Wyatt behind the checkout counter. They each look up from what they're doing and gape one by one. I'm wondering if I've already faced the firing squad—a joint decision to ask me to leave? —while my back was turned.

"Have a seat." Ms. Fax gestures to the lonesome chair across from her desk in the small and cluttered office. I'm surprised as I sit that Ms. Fax didn't ask the most generous Rockfords for a bigger office. And then I'm worried my 'firing' has something to do with running into the man who thought me just *bearable* last weekend.

Ms. Fax folds her hands. "You remember I asked you about your interest in children last week, Ms. Eyermann?"

"Oh." I kind of stumble over my words even as I breathe a sigh of relief. It's not at all what I was expecting. "Yes. Yes," I manage to say at last.

"School lets out next week." Ms. Fax shuffles the papers on her desk, not realizing she's reminding me I'm about to spend my summer with Sinjin. "And we're about to launch our summer reading program." She slides a flyer in front of me.

At least I think it's a flyer. It's certainly an attempt at getting information across, but it's lost in outdated graphics of apples and books and worms that look like something someone printed out of Microsoft Office 2000. I take it in my hands. It's dated last year.

"I'm looking for a volunteer to help coordinate this year's efforts." Ms. Fax pauses and licks her lips. "In fact, we're rather behind, and I was hoping you could make the program your primary focus from now on."

No more stuffing envelopes, no more opening mail? It's not quite shelving books, but it's certainly a step up. *And maybe it'll be an excuse not to talk too much to Sinjin.* "Sure," I say, and when I see the disgusted look on Ms. Fax's face, my smile falls. "Thank you for the opportunity," I say, all professionalism. "I'd love to help."

I slide the flyer back toward her and she nods, satisfied, grabbing a pen and starting to scribble down notes. "Good."

I'm hit with the sudden realization that if Ms. Fax oversees my work, I might be stuck in this very office, with this very sour-faced woman, for the rest of the summer between herding kids and reading books with a dozen beady eyes staring up at me. I swallow and am starting to weigh the benefits of just biting the bullet and working alongside Sinjin instead, when Ms. Fax slides a small slip of paper over to me.

She folds her fingers again. "I'll need you to coordinate your efforts with the project leader. Please do get started this weekend. As I've said, we're already behind."

I grab for the paper without breaking contact with Ms. Fax's eyes, my fingers trembling. What will I find there, some suggestions? The name of the project leader? *Sinjin's name,* I think, although I'm not sure why she'd bother writing it down for me.

"You know," says Ms. Fax. "We have an opening for a paid position as a page this fall. I'd consider your efforts here as an excellent example of your dedication to the library."

My lips twitch slightly. "Thank you." *Paid. In the fall. Of course.* I'm actually glad she seems to think it a possibility that someone who injures her favorite patron and drips water all over the library carpet might have a future with her, but it's not the time nor place to explain to her that dropping out of college to become a full-time page in the fall would be tantamount to causing Mom and Cooper separate heart attacks.

No, I have the paper to distract me. I look down. It's a phone number. Followed by the last name I'd ever think to see just now written in inhumanly perfect penmanship: E. Rockford.

Let's hope the 'E' stands for something like 'Emily' or 'Elizabeth.'

OWEN'S not feeling well enough to go to his final track and field meet, and I have to wonder if he's actually 'too ill' to attend any last-day-of-school celebrations this evening as well, or if he'll suddenly feel the touch of a miracle healer when the sun's finished setting.

Mom doesn't seem to care. She's used the cancelation as an excuse to whip-up some last-minute casserole out of leftovers, but Cooper is using the opportunity of us all sitting aimlessly in front of empty plates while we wait for Mom to drag the casserole out of the oven to lecture Owen.

"You're good at track and field, buddy. More than good."

I see Owen wince on cue at the 'buddy.' Hey, it's better than 'Junie.'

Cooper reaches over and puts a hand on Owen's shoulder. "You might even get a scholarship this year."

Owen tries to smile and kind of shifts his shoulder slightly so Cooper's hand can't reach. "Thanks," he says.

Mom swoops in to pick up Cooper's plate and Cooper shakes his head and wraps his hand around his fork. "I just think it's a shame you missed the final meet. If you can stand, you can run."

Remind me to crawl to the toilet the next time I'm puking in case Cooper expects me to run a marathon.

"It's the only meet he's missed," says Mom, putting down Cooper's plate full of casserole and grabbing her own. "June, grab your and Owen's plates, won't you?"

To be fair, she'd normally ask Owen to get his own, but she, at least, seems to believe Owen that he's not feeling well. I try to catch Owen's eye as I stack his empty plate atop mine, but he's looking at his lap—where I think I spy an LCD screen.

Cooper's fork clinks on his plate. "It could have been *the one meet* a college recruiter attended." He pauses, probably to chew, and Mom leaves the oven to join him at the table. "You can't risk a missed opportunity. One single meeting could be the difference between success and failure."

I'm mouthing the words 'success and failure' as he speaks them and I scoop the second serving spoonful onto Owen's plate. I return the plate to the not-too-sick-to-text target for the day for Cooper's ranting and slide back into my own spot.

"Owen knows that," says Mom, reaching over to squeeze Cooper's hand. She turns to do the same to Owen. "Owen! My god! No phones at the table!" You'd think he was concealing a handgun.

"*Fine!*" says Owen, slamming the phone on the table next to his plate. He picks up his fork and starts shoveling his casserole in.

Cooper is staring at Owen now, his fork halfway to his mouth. He puts it down quietly. "Don't speak to your mother like that!"

Owen grabs his glass of water and gulps it down. "Okay," he says. "I'm sorry." He doesn't sound all that sorry, not that I blame him. He puts his glass down. "May I be excused? I want to lie down."

Mom examines his plate—he made pretty short work of his dinner. "Yes, of course, honey."

Owen gets up from the table, his glass, plate and utensils in tow. The three of us remain eating in uneasy silence as I hear him rinsing them in the sink and loading them into the dishwasher. Cooper grabs Owen's phone from where he left it and I wince as he slides it into his own pocket. He doesn't look at the screen—no, he *trusts* us enough not to invade our privacy, he always says—but that doesn't stop him from confiscating it.

Of course, I mean, I was in high school the last time he confiscated mine. Surely between aiming to lead the business world and striving for perfect grades I was entitled one thing not to have to worry about.

Although it might help that I've learned not to push their limits as often as possible years ago.

"Where's my phone?" Owen's returned to the table, one hand on his waist and the other reaching out first toward Mom and then Cooper, demanding.

"If you're going upstairs to rest, you don't need it." Cooper takes a bite and speaks with his mouth full. I dart my eyes away, picking at my casserole.

"Ugh!" Owen tosses his hands up. *"Mom."*

Mom wipes her mouth with a napkin. The cheap, dime-a-dozen paper design is at odds with how elegantly she dabs at her lips. "You'll get it back when you feel better."

"This is *ridiculous*! I need—"

Cooper drops his fork to the table. The clink is too dainty to fully make his point, but he hardly needs sound effects. "Your mother and I *pay for* this phone, so we'll tell you whether or not you *need* it, young man."

"*FINE!*" There's that tone again. He stomps away from the table and up the stairs before Cooper has a chance to respond.

The clink, clink, clink of the forks on plates is punctuated by a thundering slam of a door upstairs. He's gone, but I can feel the tension Owen left behind travel down my skin, leaving goose bumps down my spine. I pick up my fork. Just a few more bites and then I can go—

"So, Junie, have you found yourself an occupation for the summer?" Cooper lays his fork across the top of his plate, a sign he's finished eating. But the way he rubs his palms together casually makes me think he's not about to get up from the table.

I chomp slower, almost wondering how I managed to chew before that moment without conscious jaw movement. I wipe my mouth and finish the bite. It's cold and too soggy. "The library," I say through muffled napkin.

Cooper tsks and looks down at the table, like the little bit of casserole on his plate is more worthy of his regard than his disappointing step-daughter. "I thought you were just filling in for a friend there."

I put my own fork atop my plate in the same position as Cooper's. "She's gone for the summer. I'm filling in for the whole season."

"Junie, it's not a paid position." He shakes his head. "It's not even a *good* position. An internship at a company, maybe, I could get behind. But there's no reason for you to blow your summer making no money *and* no connections."

Mom's still eating, cheerfully oblivious to how the anger at Owen has suddenly shifted pointlessly to me. "June likes reading," she says, as if this is new information to anyone at the table. "I'm just glad she's getting out of the house."

"Morgan, honey, reading is a hobby, not a career." Cooper keeps rubbing his palms together, and I find the sandpaper-like sound of his callused skin friction rather annoying. "I mean, there's publishing, but that's not exactly a thriving industry. And it certainly has no connections to our local library." He sighs. "I can talk to Tom about getting her—"

"The Rockfords," I blurt, and I'm not even sure why I'm saying it.

Cooper and Mom both turn to look at me, Mom with her fork in her mouth and Cooper with his hands clasped in prayer.

"I, uh—" I reach into my pocket and pull out the piece of paper Ms. Fax gave me. The piece of paper I was probably going to toss as soon as I remembered to. I smooth out the wrinkles and place it gently in the center of the table. "I'm going to work on a summer reading program with one of the Rockfords," I say, babbling. "They're this local family that—"

"Invests in half the businesses in town." Cooper grabs the piece of paper with his fingertips and pulls it closer to him. He's staring at it for way longer than it takes to read an initial, a name and a phone number. "I'd heard they donated a substantial amount to the library. I didn't realize their philanthropic efforts extended to volunteering for it."

"It does," I say, although I really have no idea. I haven't seen a Rockford at the library so far as I know since I nearly killed one. "Ms. Fax, my supervisor, is always going on about how much influence the Rockfords have over the library. And the staff."

Mom puts her own fork across the top of her plate and leans over the table slightly to get a better look at my note. Sheesh. It's a phone number and a partial name, people. "The Rockfords are the richest family in town," she says.

This is common knowledge? I didn't know people were familiar with the 'richest family in town' in the suburbs outside of Riverdale and the Lodges.

Cooper slides the note back toward me. "Hmm. Well. That could prove interesting."

I take the note back and stop myself from audibly sighing in relief. No working with Cooper over the summer. Who'd have thought Ms. Fax's incessant name-dropping would actually work out in my favor?

"I think it's sad." The statement seems so out of left field, I can't help but stare at her. Mom is up, stacking Cooper's plate atop her own. Just once I'd like to see Cooper do the same for her. It's not like Mom's a homemaker; they both spend their days outside of the house, so equal distribution of chores might be a given in any other family.

Cooper brushes some crumbs off of the table onto the floor. Great going, genius. If only you knew how to operate a vacuum, you could at least clean it up later. "Whatever their personal lives, the Rockfords could prove great connections for Junie. Hell, they're half the references people cite when applying for the big positions at my company."

I stop myself from asking if the fact that Cooper doesn't know them means he's not working in one of the 'big positions.'

"What's Mom talking about?" I ask, eager to stop myself from making some biting remark.

Cooper sighs and shakes his head, putting his palms back together. "The Rockfords practically own this town, so it makes sense that some of their, uh, *drama* makes the gossip rounds."

"Drama. I'll say." Mom's back at the table, collecting her and Cooper's glasses. "Affairs, accidents, illnesses…" She looks off into the distance, and I can see she's relishing it, like it's something she saw on *The Real Housewives*. "That whole love-across-classes thing."

Are we talking about an actual family or the plot to *Wuthering Heights*?

She walks away, leaving it at that, like I'm supposed to know what she's talking about. "Are there really *classes* in the modern age?"

Cooper pushes his chair back and stands, running a palm over the table for crumbs to knock to the floor again. "I think everything I've been telling you for years points to the fact that yes, there are." He points a finger at me. "And if you want to get out of the have-nots, you're going to have to work your way up to the haves."

I look around the kitchen, not sure a comfortable two-story house and two parents working really qualifies us as have-nots, but I suppose compared to a family that apparently owns half the town, he has a point.

"Give that Rockford a call," he says, pushing his chair in. "The sooner, the better. I want to hear that this volunteer work is going to do something to help you get there."

I pinch the piece of paper between my fingers. "Sure," I say. Guess it's time to see if all that praying that 'E' names run in the family has paid off.

CHAPTER SEVEN

My praying has not, in fact, paid off. But should I really be that surprised at this point?

"Hello," says a gruff voice. My fingers are still shaking from dialing the number.

"Hi." I clear my throat. I'm sort of squeaking. "This is June Eyermann from—"

"Who?"

"June Eyermann from—"

"I'm not interested."

I pause to digest the already terrible attempt at a conversation. "I'm from the library?" I'm asking, not telling him. I want to chuck the phone across the room.

"What? Oh."

And he just stops talking. Like I'm supposed to somehow smooth this over on my own. "Ms. Fax gave me your number. She wanted me to help you with the summer reading program. For the children." *D'uh. 'For the children.'* It sounds like I *am* collecting for some cause.

"All right," he says. "Come over now."

That wasn't exactly expected. *"The sooner, the better."* "Uh. Sure, I guess."

He rattles off an address and I scramble to grab a pen in time to write it down. And then he hangs up.

Am I going to work on a project for kids or making a drug deal with some shady criminal?

Still, that answers that question. It's not an 'Emily' or an 'Elizabeth.' It's not even some brother or cousin. I get to spend the evening talking to Mr. Bearable.

Maybe at least his dog will be happy to see me.

I freshen up in the bathroom for an unnecessarily long time. Not because I want to look my best, but because my legs are shaking and I'm not sure I can handle facing that ass.

Just get it over with. If you want to stay at the library, you need this.

I grip the bathroom handle and exhale. *I can do this.*

I let out a little scream. Owen is staring me down from the other side of the door.

"Jesus, Owen. Can't you wait in your room?"

Owen glances over his shoulder and turns back to me, whispering. "Going somewhere?"

I raise an eyebrow. "Yes. And you care because…?"

"I need a ride."

I squeeze between Owen and the door frame, escaping down the hall to my room. "Oh, no. No, Owen."

"No, Spoon, it's cool." Owen follows me into my room. I just love how he seems to think there's an open door policy on my room just because I've vacated it for most of the past year. "Mom knows."

"Okaaaaaay." I'm grabbing my phone to shove it into my purse. "And that *totally* explains why you're being so secretive about it."

Owen tucks his hands in his pockets. "I'm just going to Sinjin's for an end-of-the-school-year thing."

My phone buzzes and I tap the screen, part of me hoping Rockford took note of my number and texted back to cancel everything.

Cancel the evening's meeting. Cancel the kids' project. Cancel my current life. It's Margot, though:

Free to chat?

I bring up the keypad and let my fingers fly. "Want to explain why you were too sick to go to the final meet?" I ask as I type: *Not now, sorry. Off to work on project for library.*

Owen sighs and plops himself on the foot of my bed. I'm reminded of when we were kids and we thought sleeping over in each other's rooms was the epitome of awesome. He used to body slam himself onto my bed to 'claim it,' trying to get me to sleep on the floor of my own bedroom. "You ever get sick of their plans for you?"

A new message: *It's evening there, right? And I KNOW Sinjin's not working.*

"Hello. Have you *been* anywhere within three miles of this house the past few years?" I plop down next to him, cringing at the shrieking squeak of the springs. *Yeah, apparently Owen's trying to sneak to his place for a party. This is for summer reading.*

Owen leans forward and wrings his hands together, venting more to the wall instead of the sister who's running late. "I don't *not* like running. Just the whole meet thing… I can run without competing."

Huh, says Margot's text. *That was Everett Rockford's thing two years ago.*

I sigh. "Yeah, well, someone forgot to let Cooper know there's such a thing as not competing, so get used to it." *No comment,* I type.

Owen pats my knee a little too hard. "Great talk, sis. Great advice."

OMFG. Are you working with him on this?

I'm a little distracted. "What?" I look up from the phone screen and look at Owen as he stands, muttering. Something about how I didn't have to compete in a sport to please them. Please. He doesn't know how demanding they can be when it comes to being in college.

Yes, I type. *But please don't make this a big deal.*

Owen waves a hand at me. "Never mind."

I put the phone down. "Owen—"

He's already gone. My phone buzzes again. *So who is he today? Rochester? Darcy? How about Heathcliff?*

I slump my shoulders and type out a reply: *Good god, I hope not. The man's apparently been through enough drama already.* My fingers hover over 'send.' Owen's disappointed face echoes in my mind.

I delete what I've written and type: *Sorry, gtg.* I shove the phone into my purse and the purse strap over my shoulder.

"BE HERE. I mean here, here. Outside of the house." No reason to see Sinjin again before I have to.

"All right, all right. Geez, are you my sister or my mom?"

"I ask myself the same thing sometimes." I tap the clock display. "At 11:00 on the dot. I mean it."

Owen opens the door to get out. I lean over and latch onto his shirt like a piranha on its prey.

"What the hell?" says Owen, twisting backward.

"Owen, remember, as far as I *know*, you have Mom's permission to be here." I pinch my lips together. "And the fact that I *forgot* to mention I was giving you a ride when I told her I had to go work on my project is not going to come back to haunt me." I point to the clock again and let go. "11:00."

"Yes. 11:00. Cripes." Owen shuts the door behind him and tucks his hands in his pockets. I watch him shuffle up the darkened driveway and ring the door bell. It's dark inside the home, but when the door opens, I see flashing bright colors.

Well, I saw that he safely got to the party. And if he messes this up for me, so help me, I'll make sure he spends the rest of his life working for Cooper in my stead.

And now to stop delaying the inevitable. I fish my phone out of my purse and put it down on the seat Owen vacated, letting the

GPS app guide me from Sinjin's house to Rockford's place. I didn't street view, but after all of the talk from Mom and Cooper about how the Rockfords are to my town what Bill Gates is to the world, I thought I might be pulling up to some grand gated McMansion with endless, useless miles of yard just so they can keep neighbors from honing in on their territory. Instead I pull up to a nice gated community of condominiums. *And that would be why his address includes a unit number, genius.* Probably out of my league for life, but not Daddy Warbucks-worthy. *See, no mansion. No hidden wife locked away in the attic.*

"Hi," I say to the security guard as I roll down my window. "I'm here to see Mr. Rockford in 218?"

The security guard consults his clipboard. "Name?"

"June Eyermann."

The guard nods and pores over the list, flipping a page and looking beneath it. "Sorry. You're not on the guest list."

"The… guest list?" I'm not following. "He asked me to come over." I grab for my cell phone, weighing whether it's worth calling him again. Is he having some party? How the hell would we work on the summer reading program then? Did he forget about me? Did he completely misunderstand who I was and what I was there to do?

I want so badly just to turn around and go home. Or probably just meander around until 11:00 so it's not suspicious that I come home and go out again to pick up Owen. I'm about to slide the phone back into my purse.

"Look, lady, I can page him if you want."

What do I want? I gaze up at the security guard. *Page him?* Is this the 1990s?

I guess I'm taking too long to decide, so the guard decides for me. He clicks his tongue and shakes his head, picking up a phone and punching in a few numbers. "Mr. Rockford?" he says after a minute. "I have a Miss—" He stops and looks at me again.

"Eyermann. June."

"—Miss June Eyermann here?" He listens to the phone for a bit.

I can't even tell how much time is passing. I check over my shoulder to see if there's anyone behind me so I can start backing out.

"All right," says the guard. The gate lifts. I catch the guard's eye and he motions me through, shooting me a look that says he can't believe I'm still not getting the message. "You can *go*," he says, nodding toward the gate, and I take my foot off the brake and go through. Maybe a little too quickly.

I have no idea where I'm going. But I squint through the open window and find the numbers on the condo doors in the dim porch lights. When I find 218, then I have to worry about where to park. Because there aren't any open spots anywhere. I sigh for the benefit of no one but the apparently laughing mischief gods watching over my life and keep driving. A few minutes later, I find a spot that's probably a good five-minute walk away. Praying I won't be ticketed for taking up what might be a resident's spot, I park, grab my purse and step out.

And the sky rumbles.

Why didn't I think to check the forecast? Or to keep an umbrella in Mom's car? Not that I need to be sending any more umbrellas into people's faces.

I pump my legs and power walk down the sidewalk. I've barely made any progress when the rumbling pays off in promised sprinkles. I shift my purse over my head and start half walking/half jogging. It doesn't help. A few seconds later, it begins to pour and I still have over half the distance to cover.

When I finally run up the walk to 218, the small overhang doesn't provide much relief. I ring the buzzer. When that leads to nothing, I pound on the door.

I'm soaking wet. I don't really care right now about making a good impression.

When the leggy blonde with cheekbones so pronounced I'm wondering if her skin is two sizes too small answers, I'm worried I haven't got the right door.

"Is this where Mr. Rockford lives?" I ask. Water is gushing down my back.

Instead of letting me in or telling me I've got the wrong place so I can be on my way, the woman just stares. And stares. Then finally her lips purse a little, and she turns around.

"Ev?" she says. "Are you expecting someone… short?"

You could have just asked me for my name.

I can't see very well around the tall woman, but I don't get the impression there's a party of several dozen behind her. I'm not sure why there were no parking spaces then.

"Oh! Hello!" The cheerful greeting is not what I'm expecting. "Strange to see you here! Or maybe not so strange after all?"

It's the handsome man I stumbled into at the mall: Blake. He slides in beside the blonde woman and shoves her gently aside, gesturing for me to come in. "Get out of the rain—quickly! Isla, honestly, keeping a woman out in the gushing rain like that."

"Hello," I say as I pass. I keep my eyes down.

Blake shuts the door behind me. He and the woman—*Isla*—stare at me expectantly, Isla with her arms folded across her chest and an eyebrow raised, and Blake with his hands clasped together, a smile on his face.

"You're here to see Everett?" he asks.

I nod, bringing my purse off of my head and scrambling to find the summer reading flyer. I take it out and notice Isla regarding me like I've brought out a clump of mud. She takes a step back to avoid my dripping purse. My hand holding the flyer falters. "I'm here for the summer reading program."

"Here, let me take that. Maybe get a towel to pat it dry." Blake swoops in and grabs my purse from me before I can stop him, and I'm left standing awkwardly in the foyer with Isla, the creased flyer in my hand.

Isla looks over my head at Blake. "He's *still* doing that thing?"

"Hmm?" I turn to watch Blake appear from a hallway, a large towel over his arm, which he hands to me. "Here, dry yourself off." I tuck the flyer under my arm to grab it. Beneath the towel is a smaller one, which he uses to dab my purse with. I feel awkward rubbing my back and hair with the towel, watching someone else dry my purse like a manservant.

"I *asked*," repeats Isla, "if Ev is still doing that library thing this summer?"

Blake shrugs. "I don't know. But sure. Why not?"

Isla snorts and passes by, sticking her back as far against the entryway wall as possible as she passes. "Because it doesn't *suit* him."

If she's referring to the fact that he's too grumpy to lead a program for kids, she might have a point.

Blake sets his hand towel down on the kitchen counter and lays the purse atop it with such care, he might as well be handling a carton of eggs. He smiles at me. "I think she might be more upset about the fact that it eats up so much of his time in the summer."

I give him a faltering smile in return. Whatever Rockford's business with his wife/girlfriend/whatever—

Do friends of men who are dating someone try to get them to talk about 'pretty' girls they run into—literally—in stores?

The thought reminds me of the 'bearable' comment and I chomp down on my lip, roughly running the towel through my hair one last time.

"You're late."

I shift the towel away from my eyes slowly, bringing the whole man into view, from legs to torso to scowling face. At this point, it's sort of ridiculous that I was hoping to find someone else, but I have to admit that maybe a small part of me was hoping—I don't know, for a son named after a father? *But would a father who raised that jerk be any more pleasant to work with?*

I pull the towel away from my head, knowing full well my hair must be sticking up in all directions like I've just pulled my fingers out of an electrical outlet. "I didn't..." I clench my fists around the towel. "You didn't specify a time."

"I said to come *now*." He looks me over, and I can feel him studying my face, my wet shirt, my soaked jeans. He looks up and down twice and I'm about ready to throw the towel I'm clenching at him and make my escape like a magician with a little misdirection. "I should have known," he says, yanking me out of my fantasy. "You."

So he didn't even realize when I called I was the one who knocked him over in the last rain storm, the one whose appearance he finds so bearable? And he *still* acted like a curt jerk? Well, at least I know it's been nothing personal, if that's any consolation.

"Ev," says Blake, taking the towel from me. "Maybe part of your philanthropy this summer can be to work on your people skills a little?"

Rockford breaks his stare to glare at Blake for a second but says nothing. He turns on his heel and gestures for me—Blake? Both?—to follow. "This way."

Nice to finally properly meet you, too, jerk. Just get through this. Cooper's office. This or Cooper's office.

I take my shoes off carefully and leave them near the back door, although I don't see any other pairs.

"You don't have to worry about that." Blake is beside me, and I notice his own shoes are still on. But they're not soaking the flooring and carpet.

"They're wet," I say, not sure if it's worth arguing about.

"Why, aren't you considerate!" Blake cups his cheek with the back of his hand and whispers to me. "I think doing a little water damage to his condo might be at the top of my to-do list if he'd just spoken that way to *me*." He lays the side of his finger across his lips and stares at me. "Maybe brush before you go in, though."

Brush? Oh, my hair. I force out a sheepish laugh, toss the flyer on the counter, and grab my brush out of my purse. I run the bristles through my knotted soggy hair and do my best to tame the wheat-colored locks into something closer to human hair instead of tumbleweed. "Thanks," I say, slipping the brush back into the purse and smiling at Blake. I grab my phone out of my wet purse and slip it into my pocket before gripping the flyer again tightly like it's my invitation to be here.

"Much better!" Blake claps his hands together. "This way!" He pauses and winks at me. "Please."

I grin and follow after the tall man's back, wishing I was tasked with working with Rockford's friend instead. And wondering how on earth the two could *be* friends to begin with. Unless... Maybe he's also a Rockford, a brother or cousin. Would getting on his good side be enough to satisfy Mom and Cooper, even if I quit the reading project with his troll of a relative?

Blake peers over his shoulder as we walk down a rather large hallway. "I'm Blake, by the way. Everett's friend." He holds his hand out.

There goes that theory, and that hope. I suddenly remember Margot told me 'Everett' was the only male Rockford about his age. "June," I say, taking his extended hand and shaking.

Blake looks forward again and turns a corner. "The rather prickly doorkeeper was Isla, my sister," he continues. "Since she left before introducing herself."

Great. So he *is* related to an irritable sourpuss, but it's not the one who can help me make 'connections.' Unless... I notice he didn't introduce himself as 'Everett's brother-in-law,' but maybe that's not out of the question. Could a Rockford relative through marriage count? Or future marriage? I'm desperate here.

Blake pauses and swings his arms out to the side like one of the models on *The Price Is Right* with a showcase. I take a step into the room, a recessed living area with a modern deco fireplace in the center of a couch-circled pit. Even with the rain, it's plenty warm out despite the recent swings in temperature, so the fireplace isn't on, which makes me wonder why Rockford and Isla are gathered here in the dim overhead lights, wine glasses positioned beside them at the corners of the pit.

I have no idea where to sit. I have no idea how we're going to work on this with Blake and Isla here, but hell, it'd probably be even more awkward without them.

I fumble down the few carpeted steps and slide non-threateningly into an empty side of the couch-pit, perpendicular to Rockford and Isla, tossing the flyer beside me. Blake follows me. "June, can I get you anything? Red or white?"

I'm wondering if Blake and Rockford are roommates. "Water please. I'm underage."

Isla snorts and picks up her own wine glass, sifting its contents in a circle in front of her chest. "Like that's ever stopped anyone." She sips.

"*Isla*," says Blake, in a tone harsher than I've yet to hear from him. Not that it comes anywhere close to matching the sharpness of either Rockford or Isla in the few minutes I've known them.

Isla pulls the glass away from her lips. She's left just a touch of blood red on the clear glass. "What? *I'm* of age."

Blake shakes his head and leaves, and Isla puts her glass down on the little table at the corner. She leans an arm on the top of the couch and stares at me, raising an eyebrow while studying my face. "So are you in middle school?" She tilts her head sideways.

I half turn my head to see if she's addressing someone else, some child Rockford's had hidden in the closet. No, of course. Me. I grit my teeth. "College," I say.

Isla laughs, and it's something between derision and genuine amusement. She touches her lips lightly with rose-colored fingertips. "Oh, goodness! I'm sorry. You're so—" She waves a hand up and down over me. "—*small*. And you said you were here for Ev's summer reading program. I thought maybe he decided to enlist the help of one of the older children he reads to this year." She turns her head back and pats Rockford on the thigh. I realize he's been engrossed in his phone screen, and he doesn't so much as flinch or work up the slightest twitch of a smile at her touch.

"Violet suggested I get one of the volunteers to help me this year," he says, tucking the phone into his pocket. He hasn't commented on her 'mistaking' me for a middle schooler. He gets up and walks in front of Isla to grab his glass of wine from the table. "Where do you go to school?" he asks, suddenly like one of my parents' friends, barely interested in the fact that I'm alive, but desperately looking for something, *anything*, to say to this 'kid' they're stuck talking to.

"Chicago," I say, not feeling the need to explain exactly which school. Isla would probably twist it into some sign of my inferiority. I clutch the damp knees of my jeans awkwardly, feeling the stiffness invading my shoulders. I don't want to lean back. I can't possibly relax.

Isla looks from me to Rockford and back and must decide that since Rockford seems half interested in pursuing this topic, she's got to play along, too. She makes a fist lightly with one hand and places it under her jaw bone, probably trying to appear thoughtful. "What do you study?"

"Business administration," I spit. I can't even say the words in polite company without feeling it barb my tongue.

Rockford was about to take a sip of wine, but he pauses, peering down at me from over the glass. "How... *creative*." He finishes his sip and refuses to meet my eye any longer.

"Here you are." Blake's returned without my noticing, and he's got two glasses in hand. He holds out the plain glass of water and I take it, grateful for the moment's distraction. He sits next to me, casually putting his arm atop the couch behind me, not realizing that the action makes my heart beat faster.

Whoa, girl. Gay. I'm not interested in Blake, but I can't exactly stop myself from thinking he's hot, now can I?

"Blake," says Isla, picking back up her wine glass. I cradle my glass of water on my lap self-consciously. "Jane's a *business* major."

"June," both Blake and I correct her at once. I take a sip of water and lift the corner of my lips slightly in gratitude.

"Is that so?" asks Blake. He looks at Rockford and Isla, as if waiting for them to say more. "Isn't that what you were, Ev?"

"Among other things." Rockford finishes his glass in one last gulp.

"Everett triple-majored in school," says Isla, putting a hand proudly on his knee. "And he just finished his master's."

I nod and take another sip of my water. I have no idea how I'm going to steer the conversation to what I came to do, or if just chatting about Rockford's superior accomplishments will be enough to get my foot in the door of some business I have no interest in working in.

"I'm amazed how many people get business degrees these days," says Blake, standing to put his wine glass down. He's not saying it condescendingly like Rockford or Isla might. "There are so many opportunities in business, and so many talented people in the major."

God, I wish he were straight. Or at least my reading program partner.

"'Talented people'?" Rockford lets out a little snort that might be something like a laugh. He says nothing as Isla takes his empty glass from him and sets it down beside her own at the table. "Blake, what exactly do you mean by that?"

Blake tilts his head slightly, studying his friend sitting kitty-corner from him. "It's a popular field, but that doesn't make it an easy one. Pretty much every talented person who works with your mother lists business administration among their majors."

"*Among* their majors," says Rockford, leaning back into the couch. He puts both arms up on the top of the couch, and Isla tries to casually lean back into his arm. "You make it seem as if their talent springs from their studies. No, not everyone in the major is talented. Far from it. It's a popular 'safe' option for those who have no idea where their passion lies."

"June knows her passion," pipes up Isla, entirely unhelpfully. "It just happens to be in business, I'm sure. Business deals and marketing and all that." She nods to me and I slide the nearly full water glass onto the table.

"You're more confident in my passion than I am," I say. "I'm interested in many things, but my interests have little to do with my career plans."

"That's a pity," says Blake. "Still. College is a time to find yourself. Maybe you'll find a way to incorporate your interests into your deals and marketing."

Unless they're looking for someone to market books that have already been out for hundreds of years and seem to have no trouble selling, I doubt that.

Rockford sniffs, drawing my attention back to him. He's looking away, at the wall behind the fireplace, but there's nothing there for him to look at. "*Talented* people in the business major already do that." He turns back to look over my head at Blake. "And I have to say, I'm astonished you use my mother's companies as an example. Creativity, intelligence, skill? They're nothing but yes-men. I can't say I've met more than half a dozen talented people there in my life."

"I'm surprised you've met *any*," I say, wringing my hands. The group turns to stare at me, and I feel my smile faltering.

Rockford's gaze locks on me now. "Is your faith in your own major so low?"

I shake my head. "No. But if your standards for 'being talented' are so high, I don't think I qualify." I chew on my lip a moment. "Sometimes being a yes-man *is* a talent." I try to smile. "We can't all be Jane Austen or Stephen King. We can't all be creative and not think about how the money will follow."

"June's an aspiring author," says Isla, in the second instance of rather annoyingly trying to tell everyone what I, a person she met less than half an hour ago, am. "A struggling one, apparently."

"No," I say. "I'm not." I grab the flyer and put it on my lap. I run one of my fingers over the old book and apple graphics. "Just a book lover."

"Well, I think it's rather mean of people to look down on those who *succeed* and chalk it up to a difference in situation and not a difference in talent, as it is." Isla isn't looking at me, but there's no one else she could be talking about.

"I agree," says Rockford, as if I need more reasons to hate him. "But I have to say it goes both ways. I agree with the fact that even some talented people will go unnoticed if things don't align just right, and it's rather mean of someone to say otherwise." He squeezes his lips together in a thin line and Isla seems to sink a few inches into the couch.

I think Rockford might need to look in the mirror before he makes impartial judgments on meanness, but at least I'm satisfied that he's not a total out-of-touch rich asshole. Just a rich asshole.

"That whole love-across-classes thing." Mom mentioned something about poor people in the family.

Hmm. Well, maybe he's just offended because somebody in his family might have been born a pauper with an annual income in the measly six digits.

CHAPTER EIGHT

Okay, you're going to say I'm crazy, I type. *But I just lived a scene right out of* Pride and Prejudice. *And I don't mean any of the good ones. The one where D and L argue about "accomplished" women.*

Although it may be a bit of a stretch considering the difference in time periods and what exactly constitutes 'accomplishments,' it certainly does feel like we had the same argument. *Oh, maybe I should clarify that Rockford wasn't being sexist or anything. Just anti-human.*

Rockford, Isla and Blake—who I find out to my disappointment is *not* Rockford's roommate—have left me to the couch-pit alone, so rather than staring at the stark white and black décor with hardly a single trinket to prove there's someone living who inhabits the place, I continue the line of texts with Margot. France is six hours ahead, so she's probably sleeping by now. I don't expect a response, but I at least see what she typed after I texted her that I had to go: *You jerk! Don't leave me hanging. :D I miss all of our period dramas, so your drama is the next best thing.*

I slide the phone back into my jean pocket and do my best to smooth out the wrinkles of the flyer. What am I going to say when he gets back?

You can start with how pathetic this flyer is.

That's almost all I know about the program. I can't even picture that rather tall man sitting on that iron chair in the story time room, behind him those beautiful brush-stroked moors, his gruff voice telling children of green eggs and ham. I think he'd last about two rhymes before the children ran the other way, screaming.

"Sorry for the delay. Blake says goodbye. Again."

The tension in my shoulders that had dissipated at the thought of the story time monster reappears. Rockford crosses past me and tosses a tablet on the couch kitty-corner from me, where Isla was seated.

"It's getting a little chilly now, with the sun setting and the rain." He stares at me and then hugs his biceps as if to emphasize his point. "I'm going to start a fire." He pauses, staring, perhaps waiting for me to dare to contradict him.

"All right," I say, and he releases me from his stare at last. He drops his arm and spins, opening the screen to the fireplace.

I watch him for just a short while, adding logs from a space beneath the stone slab on which the metal-gated fireplace sits, turning knobs, sprinkling something inside the gate. Eventually, he has a pleasing, small fire going and crosses up the small staircase to dim the already-dim lighting in the room. I guess he wants the full effect of the firelight. He crosses past me and sits, picking up his tablet and working his fingers across it in silence.

I suddenly feel incredibly ill-prepared with my small-screened phone in my pocket and a crumpled flyer in my hands. Maybe I can borrow a pen. Rockford examines his tablet screen for a while longer, brushing his fingers over it.

"I'm sorry if I was interrupting a gathering," I say, just to fill the silence. *What the hell are you sorry for?! He demanded you get over here 'now'! He could have told you he was entertaining!*

"Don't worry about it." Rockford waves a hand and doesn't look up from his screen. "They're here all the time."

So they have TV- and book-less discussions with wine around a fireplace *all the time*? As if I don't already feel like a saltine cracker on a plate with prime rib and sushi. I grab for my cup of water and hold it in my hand, sipping from it from time to time just for something to do.

He works on his tablet for a few more minutes and I'm starting to wonder if he'll notice if I just let myself out when he looks up. "You're staring at me. Am I that good-looking?"

I gulp loudly, almost spitting out my water. "What? No."

"Wow." I notice the muscles in his cheek clench. "I didn't take you for someone so blunt."

"I—" I'm watching him now, but only because he's called attention to himself. I'm staring at the way his hair curls slightly over his forehead, the way his eyes are lighted up. "I'm sorry," I say, although I really shouldn't be. *'Bearable,' remember?* "I wasn't expecting a question like that." I put the glass down on the small table. "I just meant people shouldn't judge others based on appearances. Whether they're good-looking or *bearable*."

Rockford's lips twitch. "That's what people say when they actually mean they find you ugly." He leans back into the couch, picking up the tablet and resting one foot on the other knee. "It was a bad attempt at a joke. I'm sorry. But now I'm curious, exactly what is it about me you find so unappealing?"

I finger the flyer, stopping myself just short of ripping it to pieces. *Your attitude for starters.* I want to say it. I really do. I have no idea how I got into this position. *Cooper's office. Cooper's office. Networking.* I notice the flush at his cheeks in the dim glow of the fire. *He's probably had too much wine.* "Your attitude for starters." Shit. I wasn't supposed to actually say that.

Rockford hunches forward a little. "My attitude?"

"You're rather blunt yourself." I avert my gaze, staring at the wrinkled paper in my hands.

"You're right. On both accounts." I notice his foot return to the ground out of the corner of my eye. "Looks aside, you're probably more compelling than I am. Like right now." He pauses. "I've made you uncomfortable, and your eyes are focused on the floor, on that ratty old flyer, anywhere but at me. You're retreating. It makes me want to be talkative with you all the more."

I bite my lip hard. I'm wondering if this man somehow missed Human Communication 101 with all his triple majors and graduate studies. He proves himself more and more of a jerk with everything he says. I shouldn't care at all what he thinks and I don't—but the "looks aside" comment stings. Even if it is buried in half-assed compliments.

I have nothing more to say to him on this ridiculous topic and after a minute he stands, practically tossing the tablet atop the flyer in my lap. He's opened some documents with endless text under a heading titled "Summer Reading Ideas." Rockford grabs my almost-full glass of water. He stands and walks away with it. *Guess he doesn't want me to be distracted with water if I get thirsty?*

I'm too confused and angry and hurt to read more than a few sentences and then he returns, with my glass completely full, and sets it back where he found it. He only needed to add half an inch to fill it.

"Thank you," I say as he grabs a poker and opens the gate to the fire, prodding the logs. He doesn't appear to be upset that I said I don't find him good-looking. He stands there like all the world's his stage, like there's nothing anyone could do to shake his confidence. It's that confidence that keeps my eyes drawn to his face, even when I'm so upset with him.

"Sure." He grunts and shuts the gate to the fire. He turns, dropping the poker back in place. "Before we start work, I thought..." He clasps his hands together. "I'd like to learn more about you."

I meet his eyes, and I immediately regret it. I do my best to politely smile.

"Go ahead," he says, taking his seat again. "Say whatever you like."

So that you can mock me for it? Tell me how superior your own accomplishments are? I don't think so.

"I mean it." Rockford rests his foot on his knee again and bounces his knee distractingly. "I'm dwelling on rather unpleasant thoughts this evening." His smile is forceful, more off-putting than putting me at ease. "Perhaps you could distract me."

I find myself letting out a breath I wasn't even aware I was holding. *Think of it as a job interview.* I stare back at the screen, scanning the first few paragraphs in a series of documents that seems to go on and on. *Is he running a local library summer reading program or opening a school for kindergarten through 8ᵗʰ grade?* Maybe both, for all I know. Maybe they've been planning to turn the Rockford Private Library into the Rockford Private School, part of the Rockford Funded City all along.

I can feel him watching me as I continue reading, and I have to read the same sentence over and over and over. It doesn't help that it's rather long-winded. I clear my throat. "I'm wondering if you're over-thinking this. Are these all new ideas? Or did you do some of them when you ran the program previously?"

"Not that. Not yet." All of a sudden I'm holding nothing. He's yanked the tablet out of my hands and placed it on the table next to my glass of water and the empty wine glasses. "First I'd like to know about you, the person. Say something."

I'm entirely at a loss. I stare at him and feel his dark eyes looking for answers an hour ago I wouldn't have even conceived he'd be interested in knowing if someone had paid him to ask me. "How's your ankle?" I venture, stupidly. But I'd rather he remember how poorly our first meeting went than this. I feel uncomfortable in his sudden interest.

"Fine now."

"Where's your dog?"

"He's not mine."

I've officially run out of things to say.

He sighs and shakes his head, finally ceasing the endless bouncing of his knee.

"If you want to have a conversation," I say, my irritation rising, "it'd help if you asked some questions. I don't know what you want to know about me. I don't know what interests you at all."

"All right," he says, sliding his foot back to the floor. He leans forward, his arms on his legs. "You're a business major volunteering at the library. You're still in college and you're not passionate about your field of study. Would you agree at least that since I'm a bit older than you, since I'm more educated, since you're working under me for the summer reading program, that I have the right to lead the project?"

I'm not sure why I'm even here, if he thinks he has all the answers. "It's not up to me."

He turns to catch my eye. "That's not an answer. Unless it's your intent to be vague, which is probably more annoying. Say what you think."

If I say what I think, I'll lose this opportunity. I do so anyway. "I don't really care who leads this project. And I don't know what I'm doing here if it's not to brainstorm with you how to fix it, even if you have the whole thing planned out." I point to the tablet. "But I will say this: I don't think you being a little older and more educated than me means you're somehow more qualified than me."

He snorts. "You have a point—you don't need much to lead a volunteer project, but I have to disagree that I'm not more qualified. I just wanted to be sure, well... That you wouldn't be offended if I direct the project."

Cooper's office. Cooper's office. I smile, and I keep the smile plastered on my face, although it hurts. "It never occurred to me that I would lead this project. But thank you for concerning yourself with your underling's feelings." I'm hit suddenly with this feeling of déjà vu.

He picks up his tablet. "All right," says Rockford, examining the screen. The familiarity falters a little. "Then let's discuss my ideas for the program."

His "ideas for the program" take him a full hour to relay.

"I didn't realize this program was so complex," I say when he at last finishes reading his documents aloud.

"I was asking you for your ideas." The corner of Rockford's lips twitch.

"That *is* my idea," I say. "Simplify."

Rockford slides his tablet onto the small table. "Go on."

I do. I explain to him that choosing a theme, selecting the books to read, and focusing on the 'marketing'—how terrible the flyer is, or the in-library display—should make for a fun enough program. The questions he hopes to pose to the children after each book is read seem too rigid, the reasoning he gives for the betterment of children's education needless—we're not trying to prove the program's worth to anyone. Rockford listens, not moving his eyes from me. It's me who has to look away from time to time, focusing on the fire, the floor, his hands clutching his raised crossed legs.

At last I let the silence fall, and it hangs between us a moment, before Rockford begins to speak. "You seem very young."

I'm not sure what that has to do with the point at hand, but I'm not trying to hide my age. "I'm nineteen."

Rockford lets something like a sigh pass through his lips and he leans back. "To be young and optimistic again."

I raise an eyebrow. "You don't seem that old yourself. And you're the first person to call me an optimist. I'd prefer to speak of myself as practical."

"Practicality is nothing to strive for," says Rockford, suddenly caught up in staring at the fire's flickering. "It comes in time— along with regret. Live while you're young. Demand happiness out of every day, even if you have to throttle it."

"You make yourself sound many more decades older than I think you are."

Rockford sighs and puts both feet on the ground. "I certainly feel many more decades older." He examines me, and I look away. "I sense something of a passion behind your work at the library, one your *practicality* keeps hidden away. Don't lead a life of regret."

I chew the inside of my cheek. "I think *throttling* happiness out of my life will cause more pain than joy."

"How would you know? Have you even tried?" He makes a tsking sound and shakes his head. "Young and optimistic. And naïve."

Yeah, try growing up in my household, without buckets of cash behind you, and see how well following your passions turns out. "I'm not the one who talks about regretting something when only in my mid-twenties."

"Who says I regret something in particular?" Rockford studies me now, and I'm almost positive I've struck a nerve. "I only mentioned general regret."

Neither of us speaks for a while, and somehow we're both locked into each other's gazes.

My pocket vibrates and I rip my eyes from Rockford's. *It's too early for a message from Margot,* I think. *But she'd probably love to hear the scene I think I'm living now. Because this is just like a conversation Jane and Rochester once had.*

I look at the screen, but it's not a text from Margot. It's from Owen: *Hello? Late much?*

The phone reads 11:20. "Oh crap!" I say, and I scramble to stand. "I have to go."

Rockford moves to stand as well. "I hope you're not leaving because I've scared you away."

"No." I shake my head. "I have to pick my brother up."

Rockford looks away. "Oh." He clears his throat and looks back at me. "I'll think about what you suggested. Text me your email address and I'll forward you the revisions before Monday."

"Okay." I'm not sure if a strange conversation and listening to Rockford prattle on and on is exactly what Ms. Fax had in mind when she asked me to help plan the program, but I don't intend to argue. *I'm here for a good recommendation. I'm here for the books. I'm not here to make friends. Especially not with someone who insults me behind my back—and looks down at me even to my face.*

Even if I can't stop thinking about his wet shirt clinging to his chest that day from the rain.

I scramble up the small set of stairs and speed-walk down the long hallway. I slip into my shoes by the front door and grab for my purse on the counter.

Rockford's hand is already on the purse and I accidentally lay my palm atop his hand. It feels softer than I expected, and I can't will myself to pull away.

"June," he says, saying my name for the first time. "I... I'm sorry if I appeared blunt. People are always telling me I'm too blunt."

"It's fine," I lie, letting my hand fall. He hands me the purse and I take it.

"No, it isn't." Rockford slips his hands into his pockets. "I'm not usually this way with people I hardly know. I just... find it hard to be formal around you."

Perhaps because the first time I met you I practically tossed an umbrella in your face?

I nod curtly and do my best to smile, but it's hard to move my facial muscles. I scramble to think of what to do, and I settle for extending my hand for a shake. "I'll see you next week, then, Mr. Rockford."

"I see *you* have no trouble with formality." He gazes at my hand for too long and then takes it, shaking it a couple of times before stuffing his hand back into his pocket. "I hope it won't always be that way."

I turn around so he won't see me widen my eyes in equal parts puzzlement and disbelief. *Bearable*, I remind myself as I grab for the door handle, open the door and walk away.

Owen's sitting on Sinjin's front porch, his hands clutched to his shoulders. He pops up as soon as I pull up, running down the walkway, across the grass, and to the car.

He opens the door. "Finally!" He shuts the door and messes with the temperature knobs, blasting up the heat to full. "11:00, June? Be *outside* at 11:00?" He rubs his hands together in front of the air vent.

"All right, all right. I messed up." I lift my foot off of the brake and go.

Throttling happiness out of the day. I think of my bizarre discussion with Rockford in front of the fire. *Rochester and Jane exchanged the same strange type of thoughts in front of a fireplace.* I shake my head to clear it and focus on seeing through the fog rolling over the suburban streets. *I'm reading something fun and fluffy this weekend. Something contemporary.*

It might be time to give my favorite classics a well-deserved break since I can't get them out of my brain.

CHAPTER NINE

It's Wednesday at the library and I've made it through one and a half long days working practically inseparably from the man—*boy*—straightening magazines on the rack beside me. At least most of the tasks we have to do are in the quieter parts of the library, so there's an excuse not to be talking. And at least I found out he only plans to volunteer three days a week this summer.

If I weren't certain it would lead to Cooper and Mom remembering I'm not doing anything 'of worth' this summer, I might do the same. Between the librarians and the pages, there's not a lot left over for the volunteers to do. I imagine the program is perfect for someone who works full-time and wants to help out a few hours a week. I'm not even sure why they have a full-time volunteer shift in place.

Except to 'assist' program coordinators who have little need for input.

I spent yesterday redecorating the display case in the entryway, emphasizing Rockford's selected theme of fantasy and adventure. I found a dragon stuffed animal among the ones dotting the story time room wall and crafted a cutout of a sword and shield out of construction paper. It took me most of the day, and I think it looks a lot better, a lot more dynamic. Ms. Fax nodded when she looked at it, so I suppose that counts as approval.

But what will Rockford think?

Today's the first story time, the crux of our summer reading program. I texted Rockford my email the next day, and I got a copy of his in-depth program plan that night. It was a lot simpler than the one he'd shown me earlier. But I was still nervous I was apparently way underestimating this thing. I thought it was a matter of choosing a book and reading it.

"Ms. Eyermann, Mr. Ravi." Ms. Fax appears behind the magazine rack, curling her finger slightly. She turns, and Sinjin and I exchange a glance and follow. Ms. Fax takes us behind the administration desks—usually a no-go zone for we volunteers—and stops at a shelf in the back, pulling out construction paper, safety scissors and a stack of pencils. "Mr. Rockford said you'd be needing these this afternoon, Ms. Eyermann," she says, her voice slightly louder now that we're away from the patrons. Right, the arts and crafts portion of the after-story activities. "Mr. Ravi, I wonder if you might help Ms. Eyermann get set up before you leave for the day? Mr. Rockford can't make it."

I freeze, my hand atop the stack. "What?"

Ms. Fax pinches her lips and clasps her hands together. "Mr. Rockford can't make it this evening. You'll have to lead the first activity alone."

I reach into my pocket and pull out my phone. Nope, no messages. No apologies.

Did you really want to spend the afternoon and evening with him anyway?

No, but I didn't want to be left to run this apparently prestigious activity all alone, either.

"I do hope you think you can lead the activity on your own," says Ms. Fax, fumbling through a drawer and pulling out a dozen glue sticks. "As you know, we have no full-time children's librarian, and I can't spare anyone to help. That's why I've left this up to volunteers in the past."

Sinjin straightens the stack of construction paper and grabs the pile, laying the glue sticks on top of it. "I can stay late and help." He's watching me, probably waiting for approval.

I really can't find any reason to say no. I don't even know if I want to say no, awkwardness or not. "Thank you," I sputter, shoving the phone into my pocket and dangling the multiple pairs of safety scissors from my fingers.

Sinjin grins. "Sure. The picture book room?"

"What? Oh. Yes." I try to access the plan for the day in my brain, but I can't even remember the book. Rockford seemed so on top of things. I pull my phone out with the one hand not dangling dull scissors from each finger to check the document and move to follow Sinjin.

"Ms. Eyermann, one moment!"

I pause and watch Ms. Fax retreat into her office. I'm trying to think of what else I'm missing—didn't Rockford even lay out 'all the materials needed' in one page of his plan?—when she returns, her hand clutching a little girl's. The girl is watching me beneath the tips of slightly-too-long brown bangs, clutching a picture book to her chest.

Ms. Fax looks from the little girl to me. "This is Addy. Mr. Rockford's niece."

I shove the phone back into my pocket and wave. "Hello." *Where's your uncle?* I want to say, but those round brown eyes are so innocent, so unlike her uncle's, I can feel some of my panic melting away.

"Addy, this is Ms. Eyermann." Ms. Fax drops Addy's hand and gently pushes her forward. "He dropped her off so she can attend story time. Do you mind watching her, since you're so good with children?"

He was here. And he couldn't even track me down to apologize?

Addy walks over to my side and reaches for my hand, her bangs tumbling away from her eyes as she cranes her neck back to gaze up at me. And I suddenly find it *is* possible to panic in the face of those wide brown eyes.

———

"ADDY, do you want me to find you markers or crayons?" Sinjin looks over the little girl's shoulder at the piece of construction paper she's doodling on with a pencil.

Addy grins and meets Sinjin's eyes. "Yes, okay!"

The children's book room is still fairly empty, with some parents and their kids browsing through the bins of books. Some leave almost immediately, but some seem to be lingering, probably ready for story time even if it's still half an hour away. I'm flicking through Rockford's documents on my phone, getting less confident the more information I try to recall.

"June, I'm gonna go see if Violet has some markers."

I look up from the phone briefly, offering Sinjin a faltering smile. He leaves, and I'm stuck against the faux moors trying to make sense of what I'm doing. I let out a deep breath and put the phone down on the iron wrought table. At least I managed to pull out the books he selected from the collection even before I knew my role for the day wouldn't be blissfully confined to supporting from the shadows.

Addy is staring at me, the eraser of her pencil tucked between her lips. I try to smile and walk over to her, taking a look at the paper. She's drawn several stick people and something that looks like a balloon animal blob. "What are you drawing?" I ask.

"Captain." Addy points to the balloon animal blob.

"Captain!" I say, pulling out a tiny chair at the kids table and sitting down next to her. "Is he your dog?"

Addy's face lights up. "Yes!"

"I've met him," I say. "We both got soaked in the rain."

Addy laughs and gets up from her chair, spinning in place. "He can do this!" She gets louder as she spins again. "I say 'dance' and he spins!"

"Addy, stop." I reach a hand out to try to stop the twirling little madwoman, conscious of all the eyes boring down on us from around the room. She stops and almost tumbles. I get up to guide her back into the chair. She can't stop laughing. "That's great." I point at the drawing, eager to get her off topic before she starts showing me how he can bark on command. There's a little stick figure and big stick figure. "Is that you and your mom?"

"That's my *uncle*," she says, and she picks up the pencil she dropped on the table. She connects the two stick figures with two stick figure arms. She stops. "Why couldn't he stay?"

I raise my eyebrows. *That's what I want to know.* "I don't know. I wish he was here. He was going to read." Although I can't picture that at all, it's better than picturing myself doing it in a few short minutes.

"He never does what he promises." Addy puts her pencil down and pouts, kicking her leg.

I wish I could do the same.

"Here you go, Addy." Sinjin's returned, a box of crayons in hand. He looks at me. "We should have had those for the event anyway."

"I think it's on the prep list." I get up and walk over to my phone.

"June, seriously?" Sinjin's crossing his arms over his chest in a really cute way, and I can't look for more than two seconds. "You need to consult a list for crayons?"

"No, you're right." I shake my head. A screech from the entryway draws my attention and two small boys run down the walkway between the bins of books to jump on the cushions in the story time corner.

"Shh!" Sinjin lifts a finger to his lips. "Boys, you have to be quiet in the library." He crouches down beside them. "That's how you win the secret library game."

The boys exchange a look and giggle, but they cover their mouths to muffle the sound.

A weary-looking mother, I assume, traipses in after them,

sweatshirts piled over her arms, a purse strap continuously falling off her shoulder. "I'm so sorry!" she says to Sinjin and me.

"It's no problem." Sinjin stands and beams, and the tension melts out of the woman's face. "We'll take good care of them."

If I didn't know better, I might think the woman was in love.

God, he knows the right thing to say to everyone. I feel so much better. He's saved my ass. Story time with Sinjin is bound to be a million times more appealing than what uptight Rockford had in store.

"THANK YOU FOR COMING! OH!" I scramble to the little crafts and arts table and pick up a construction paper dragon's head with a forked tongue three times its length. "Don't forget your dragon!"

The little boy trots back and grabs the cardboard cutout from me, and runs back to the mom who left him with us for an hour, grabbing her hand. She looks like she got a full spa treatment just by having a little me-time by herself elsewhere in the library. *The power of quiet reading.*

The woman looks up from complimenting her son's dragon, locks eyes with Sinjin and stumbles, trying awkwardly to recover as she exits the story time room.

Or the power of hot jailbait.

I stack the construction paper scraps for recycling, watching Sinjin collect the glue and scissors out of the corner of my eye. He doesn't pass for a high schooler, especially not when he's dressed like it's casual day at the office. And he doesn't walk around asking stupid questions like "Am I that good looking?" either, unlike some people hardly worth mentioning.

"That went great, June!" Sinjin collects the leftover pieces of construction paper and shows off his incredibly white set of teeth. "Did you have a nice time, Addy?"

Addy's the last kid left in the room, and she's browsing through a collection of picture books about dogs that Sinjin helped her find when she refused to make a dragon after I read the story her uncle picked. "Hmm." Addy nods, clearly not paying us much attention.

Sinjin and I exchange a look and laugh. It feels nice. It almost feels normal.

I clear my throat, shuffling and straightening my pile of scraps again and again. "Thank you so much for helping me out, Sinjin."

"I was happy to." He offers to take the pile of scraps from me, and he stacks them atop the rest of the paper, the glue and the scissors. "Despite working together, I don't really feel like we've been working *together*, you know? We haven't really talked."

"Oh? Yeah." I laugh nervously, trying my best to seem like I hadn't noticed that. "Ms.—Violet keeps us so busy." I peer over his shoulder to make sure Ms. Fax didn't hear me say that. I pinch my lips for a moment, but then I decide to go for it. "But you really helped me out. Do you… Do you need a ride home or something? I kept you late."

Sinjin suddenly loses his grip on his pile of arts and crafts and stumbles to catch it. I swoop in to help, pushing the pile back against his chest. My hand brushes his arm, and we peer into each other's eyes. I smile, breaking eye contact first. "Let me," I say, scooping the glue sticks out of his pile and sliding the safety scissors over my fingers again.

"Yes." Sinjin's agreement is so sudden, I pause, not sure what he means. He clears his throat. "I mean, thank you, yes. Rather than wait for the next bus—"

I smile. "You and Owen really need to get those licenses."

Sinjin's eyebrows arch. "I have a license. Just don't have a car. Yet. I'm saving."

"Well, look at you." I pull away, one hand clutching a few cylinders of glue sticks, the other dangling scissors. "All grown up in the last year."

Sinjin laughs. "You don't know the half of it."

Yikes. My mind goes *there*. A certain place we never got. I'm suddenly not sure I want to know.

"Addy, come on," I say, waving a glue stick-filled fist at her. "Take your books. I'll bring you to Ms. Fax's office."

Speak of the devil. "Ms. Eyermann, good!" Ms. Fax appears in the entryway, her hands already clasped together. "The children seemed quite engaged during the story." She peeked in briefly while I read, causing me to accidentally skip a page and have to go back, but I guess she didn't notice the mishap. "The noise levels were appropriate. Well done! I'm so glad I picked you for the task. And thank you, Mr. Ravi."

"Thank you." It's all I can say. I'm still shocked from hearing such overt praise.

"You came here in a car, correct?"

The question seems so out of place, I'm frozen. One of the safety scissors falls from my fingers and I bend to pick it up. "Yes… "

"Good!" Ms. Fax claps her hands together. "I'm wondering if you might drop off Addy at her uncle's? He said you'd been there before, and he left a booster seat so you'd be able to take her."

"Uh…" Wait, what?

"Excellent!" She turns on her heels. "Just finish cleaning up in here and you may go."

I look at Sinjin and he shrugs. "They're Rockfords," he whispers, looking over his shoulder at Addy. She's stacking her picture books together, taking some out of the pile and tucking them under her arm. "They don't ask."

And that somehow means the library employees are their personal staff? I think suddenly of Jane becoming Adèle's governess.

Thinking I'm living in a book is probably a sign that my life is headed in the wrong direction.

CHAPTER TEN

If Mom's car didn't have two rows of seats, I might have gotten away with not taking Addy home. But then I figure Sinjin would be the one stuck waiting, not her, not if I valued my free labor position at the Rockford Private Library. If Mom didn't let me use her car, if she didn't frequently carpool with Cooper anyway, I might have been stuck with the bus myself.

But then I wouldn't be on my way to Rockford's with a six-year-old in a booster seat and my former sort-of-boyfriend in the back, acting like more of the perfect picturesque uncle than Rockford could ever be.

"Che-low," says Sinjin. He's been having Addy read aloud to him and only stepping in when she stops. "It's like a big violin."

"Cello," repeats Addy. "The dog wove under the man's legs and bumped into his cello."

"We're almost there," I say to the rearview mirror, more to Sinjin than to Addy. "He doesn't live far."

"Cool," says Sinjin, and he turns back to the book with Addy.

I'm kind of feeling like a third wheel in my own car.

I pull up to the security guard's checkpoint and brace myself for another argument, but surprisingly, he doesn't even have to consult his list to know I'm on it. I guess Rockford really does want to get his niece back.

There's a parking spot near Rockford's condo this time, and I'm thankful I don't have to drag a little girl for a long walk. And that the skies have managed to smile upon me for one evening and decided not to let the rain fall.

"Captain!" says Addy as I open the car door. I don't even have time to brace myself before the dog's nose is in my crotch, and he's practically crawling onto my lap to get to his little master.

"Captain!" This voice is much deeper, and much less happy. It only has to speak the dog's name a few more times before the dog finally gives up and turns back, running to Rockford's side on the walkway between the condo and the curb.

Rockford's condo door is wide open. Isla is clearly visible with a wine glass in hand and a skirt that has no business being so far above the knees. She's lingering back a little, seemingly both eager to be seen without it seeming like she's *trying* to be seen.

Is this *why he couldn't make it?*

"June!" Rockford's voice is almost as stern as it was with Captain. "Why are you here?"

Uh… I step out of the car. "I brought Addy over." I clear my throat and shut the door behind me. "After the story time summer reading kick-off event. At the library."

I open the door to find Addy already scrambling out of her seatbelt. "Uncle Ev!" She jumps out and hugs Rockford's legs. Captain barks and dances excitedly.

Rockford smiles, but he looks like he's smiling through pain. He pats her back quickly. "Head on inside." I suppose he can't really ask her how the event went in front of me. That would mean acknowledging he totally blew me off.

I watch Addy and Captain head up the walkway to the condo, and Isla retreats out of sight. I turn back to the car and Sinjin's getting out of it, Addy's books in his arms. My fingers fumble at releasing the booster seat, and I turn to hand it to Rockford.

"I'm sorry about—Oh." Rockford stops himself from continuing. He grabs the seat from me, his eyes on Sinjin as he slips around the car to stand beside me.

"These are Addy's," says Sinjin, matter-of-factly. He piles the books on top of the seat. Rockford stares at him like he's an alien.

I slam the back door and turn to face Rockford, my arms crossed. "Sinjin helped me with the story time event."

"Oh. Thank you." Rockford glances between Sinjin and me. "Do I know…?" He doesn't even finish the sentence.

"Sinjin Ravi." Sinjin reaches his hand out to shake Rockford's and then realizes Rockford has no hands left to shake. "We've met at the library before."

"Right." Rockford shuffles the pile of things in his arms to get a better grip. Then he doesn't say anything. Instead, he stares at me. Hard. And with furrowed brows. Like I'm the one with something to apologize for, and he's waiting for me to say it.

I'm not sticking around staring at the guy who seems to have confused me for some form of servant. "Well," I say to Sinjin. "Should we get going?"

Sinjin glances at Rockford and nods. "Sure." He steps behind the car to enter the front passenger seat. I put my hand on the front door handle and am about to pull.

"June." I hear the pile of books scrape against the booster seat as a hand clutches my arm.

I turn and stare up at him. I'm hoping my face expresses some of the anger I'm feeling without being so antagonistic that I'm blowing my shot at the power of this man's 'connections.'

Rockford loosens his grip. "Violet was supposed to bring Addy for me." He clears his throat and drops his hand, wrapping both arms around the pile again. "I wouldn't have asked it of you—"

"Yeah, well, Ms. Fax would definitely ask it of me." I chew my lip and look down. "Things went well today, I think. You can ask Addy."

"That's great!" He's practically smiling, but then he clears his throat and his face becomes a scowl again. "Did you follow the plan?"

I pinch my lips together. "I read the book you selected. We did the activity." I glance back into the car to see Sinjin watching us, confused. "I didn't follow the plan to the letter, but it went well."

"There's a reason why I included so much in the plan—"

I open the car door. "Then maybe you should show up next time."

I get in and close the door behind me before I can change my mind.

"What do you think kept him from coming?" asks Sinjin as I start up the car. Making sure Rockford has moved out of the way so I don't have to add "manslaughter of most generous Rockford" to my CV, I put the car in reverse.

I get a glance of Isla through the open door. She steps into view just as Rockford heads inside.

"I don't know," I say, "but I'm guessing his girlfriend might have had something to do with it."

I might be imagining things, but I swear I hear Sinjin exhale deeply as I shift into drive.

* * *

Cooper had to go back to work after dropping Mom off—some big project deadline so important the fate of the world rests on his shoulders to hear him tell it—so for once, we're not having an interrogation at dinner. For once, we can stuff our faces with gooey, melty pizza and Mom can lean back on the couch and put her feet up after working a long day.

We're watching a movie. Mom doesn't like period dramas, but she can't resist *Bridget Jones' Diary*. I don't think she remembers it's a *Pride and Prejudice* re-telling even after I've told her a few times, or that such swoon-worthy romance exists in stories from more than a few decades ago. But normally I'd take what I can get. Today I'm tired of thinking of Rockford every time I see Colin Firth's face.

"You guys watching this *again*?" Owen's down for his third

plate of pizza. Why Mom doesn't just order him his own whole pizza, I can't say.

Mom laughs like she's been caught with her hand in the cookie jar. "That's what I say every time I walk into your room. You're playing this *again*?"

"Mom, playing a video game more than once is not like re-watching a movie." Owen speaks between massive chews of the pizza he's crammed into his mouth. "Or re-reading the *same old books*."

I take another slice of grease-on-crust from the box and marvel at how quickly we've reduced the meal to cardboard stains and crumbs. "If you must know, I read *The Great Dragon Rescue* today."

"Sounds compelling." Owen folds the last bite of his slice and stuffs it into his mouth. He doesn't really sound impressed. "So much more interesting than games." He grabs two more slices and slips back up the stairs.

"Is that the children's book for the summer reading program?" Mom's eyes are glued to the TV, but she tilts her head slightly to let me know she's talking to me. "How did that go?"

"The guy who was supposed to be leading me didn't show up." I put the crust of my slice down. I'm not really a fan of cold pizza.

"The guy?" Mom looks at me out of the corner of her eye. "The... *Rockford* guy?"

"Yeah." I'm wiping my fingers on my napkin and resisting the urge to wipe the bridge of my nose along with it. What is it about good pizza that makes your skin leak practically immediately? "He dropped his niece off but couldn't bring himself to stay. Yet he was home when I dropped her off a few hours later."

"That doesn't surprise me." Mom licks her fingers and puts down her paper plate. "The Rockfords are always juggling this or that. They can hardly be counted on to make an appearance lasting more than a few minutes."

"Sure." I'm starting to wonder why Mom thinks she knows so

much about the Rockfords, and if she does know so much, why I have to forge this networking connection myself instead of through her or Cooper. But right. If I didn't, then I'd be stuck working with Cooper.

"You dropped off his niece?" Mom picks up her napkin and wipes off her hands. "So that's the second time you've been to his place."

And hopefully the last. "I didn't go in this time."

"Still." Mom shoots me a smile. "He trusts you."

Better not tell her he expected my supervisor to drop off the kid.

"Well, let's hope his niece gives him a good report." I stare pointedly at Renee Zellweger and her too-sickeningly-cute-to-be-real oh-so-clumsiness. Elizabeth Bennet Bridget Jones ain't.

"Have you asked him about job opportunities?" Mom's staring at the movie, too, but I check her out of the corner of my eye to see how casual the question is. Without Cooper around there's a chance she's just curious to know. But there's a chance she's gathering Intel, too.

"I thought of this more as a networking opportunity." I pull out my phone just for something to occupy my hands with. "Forge a working relationship with him now, and he'll have my back in three years after I graduate." *Assuming I wind up working anywhere near here. And if I do, it better not be with Cooper.*

"Oh, yeah, I can see that."

We lapse into a few moments of silence when my phone vibrates. A text message. I figure it's from Margot, so I click on it, but it's from Rockford: *I'm sorry about today. Addy says she had a great time.*

That's it. Well, I can't really expect more. And I'm glad to hear I passed the test, even without sticking to every minute detail of his plan outline. I'm about to put the phone away, figuring I can respond later and not seem like I'm constantly waiting on the phone for someone to talk to me.

"Owen admitted you took him to Sinjin's party the other night."

My hand freezes halfway to the table. "He told me you gave him permission to go."

Mom rolls her eyes. "You believed that?"

"Well, I..."

"It's fine." Mom nods. "I didn't want him to have to miss out. It's just that I had to cover for him all night. I said he was sleeping. You know, I—"

My phone buzzes again, and I suddenly remember it's in my hand: *Would you like to entertain Addy at a country club function this weekend?*

"Who's that?" asks Mom, her eyes flitting between the TV and my phone. "Oh! I think your father's home!" She cranes her neck to peer around the recliner and out the window at the driveway.

She says that sometimes. "Your father." She means Cooper. Who would kill me if he heard I turned down the offer to do *anything* for a Rockford, even if it's for free. Who would doubly kill me if he found out I took Owen out that night he was 'sick.' Better to distract him by being a good little go-getter.

Guess I'm going pro on this whole nanny/governess volunteer thing.

CHAPTER ELEVEN

"I have zero 'shiny new dresses' to wear, Margot." I stop doing the whole twirling-on-the-catwalk thing in my room in front of my phone propped up on the table. "And no, I don't think the spaghetti-strap floor-length gown with sparkles I wore to senior prom is country club attire."

Margot snorts. "Every girl needs shiny new dresses for events like these, June."

"Not every girl is spending her summer working for free."

Margot rolls her eyes. "Come off it. You told me yourself the library gig beats working for Cooper."

I plop down on my bed, the skirt of the simple short-sleeved black dress I have on riding up my legs a little bit. Margot laughs as I readjust the material. "Okay," I say, "so it might be just a tiny bit too small." Mom got it for me a few years ago because "every woman needs a little black dress." I wore it to Grandpa's funeral and a breakfast luncheon Mom's business had that year and then forgot about it.

Margot shrugs and picks up a wine glass. I'm not going to bother asking if it's real wine. "Don't look at me. I don't think your Rochester will complain if your dress is too tight."

I brush off the insinuation that Rockford would be at all interested in what I'm wearing. "So today he's Rochester?"

"You're the one who told me the whole take-care-of-Addy-for-me thing reminds you of Jane taking care of Adèle for Rochester."

I shake my head. "I was joking. For Jane, it was a *job*. And Adèle was the oh-so-precocious French maybe-Rochester's-daughter born out of wedlock, not his niece who loves drawing and her dog. And Sinjin."

Margot practically spits the yellowish drink she has floating in her wine glass. "*Everyone* loves Sinjin, don't they?"

"*Everyone* might be a slight exaggeration." I pretend-pout. "Although he did really steal the show from me when it came to the kids' moms at story time."

Margot slams her glass down on the table in front of her. "Sinjin has always impressed *older* women." She winks exaggeratedly.

"Stop trying to set me up with your brother." The words are out before I even consider what I'm saying.

Margot points to me through her phone's camera. "*You* said it, not me!" She faux-dramatically flips her hair. "And then you go and fall for a jerk brought to life from one of your ancient stories."

"I haven't *fallen* for anyone this summer." I cross my arms. "So *anyway*, you have any plans for this week?"

"Same old, same old." Like there's a 'same old' in freaking *France*. Margot looks off screen and answers a question I didn't hear anyone speak. "Yeah. June."

I chew the inside of my cheek. Unless her host mom remembered my name from the one video chat we've had a few weeks ago, there's only one person there who'd know me by name.

"Hello." Deana pulls out a chair next to her twin sister's and deigns to give me a cursory nod through the phone camera. Then she's staring off at something off camera, a glass of red wine poised sophisticatedly in her hand before her chest. *Oh, brother. Stop trying to pose for the "Beautiful college girl in France with wine" stock photo.*

Margot's eyes dart from her sister beside her to me halfway across the globe. She shrugs just slightly.

I clear my throat and decide to be the better person. "How have you enjoyed France so far, Deana?"

"It's fine." She takes a sip, then resumes looking off at something I can't see. From where I'm sitting, she looks like she's staring at my pile of dirty laundry.

"'Kay." I slip my hands under my thighs and avert my gaze.

"Margot tells me you have an overactive imagination this summer."

"I didn't say *that!*"

I turn back to look at the screen and Deana is staring me down, her lips in a thin, unnatural line. "Seeing your fictional boyfriends everywhere you go? Sounds like an overactive imagination to me."

"Oh my god, June, I did *not* say you saw fictional boyfriends everywhere you go—"

"No, it's all right." I make a point of getting up and reaching across the phone to the table to grab the gold chain my dad gave me the last time I saw him, sometime five years ago. I slip it around my neck and smile awkwardly, although I'm doing my best to seem as poised and confident as the twins do, drinking wine in the city of love. "I have to do *something* to make my summer entertaining. Since you two went off to France without me."

Margot starts to say something. "June—"

Deana takes a gulp from her wine and slams her glass next to Margot's. "Well, maybe if you'd spoken more than two words to me last semester, I might have told you about my plans."

Margot puts a hand on her arm. "Deana—"

"Deana, *you* were the one who stopped talking to me!" I don't want to look at the screen, but I do, and Deana is kind of half looking at me and half looking away. I sigh. "I'm sorry I didn't want to go to all those parties. I had work to do."

Deana shakes her head. "You don't have work to do 24/7 your freshman year of college."

"Maybe you didn't, but I did!" I pick at a small hole in my comforter. "I sucked at my classes." I take a deep breath. "You knew I didn't like my major."

"So why don't you change majors?" The way Deana says this, it's like she's telling someone who's cold to put on a sweater. "That's what I told you half a year ago, and you didn't listen."

"My parents would kill me is why." I look into the phone and lock eyes with Deana. I see poor Margot out of the corner of my eye backing her chair up warily, shut out from the conversation.

Deana shrugs. "So what? What's the worst they can do?"

"Not help pay for my college education." I chew the inside of my cheek. "Kick me out."

"You think you'd be the first person with that problem?" Deana drums her fingers on the table in front of the phone's camera. "Go to a cheaper school. Drop out for a few years and save working a full-time job. That's what I'm doing."

"But—what?"

"Deana, what are you talking about?" Even Margot's gotten in on the conversation.

Deana looks at her sister and then back to me. Her shoulders slide up and down again. "School's not really for me. When I get back at the end of the summer, I'm going to find something else to do."

Margot puts a hand on her forearm. "But Mamma and Dad—"

"They'll have to understand." Deana's staring straight through me, trying to say something without speaking, something I don't think I'm getting. But something I'm dying to understand.

I look away. "There's a full-time page position opening at the library this fall."

"Huh." I look up to see Deana nodding, looking off behind the camera. "I just might apply. Thanks."

"Sure."

"You certain you want me for competition?"

"I'm not going to apply—"

Deana smiles devilishly. "I mean for your fictional boyfriend."

I raise my eyebrows and shake my head, but I can't help but smile just a bit. Whatever nervousness Margot felt at her sister's admission, looking back and forth between Deana and me, she at least looks relieved now.

Maybe I'm feeling a bit better, too, after seeing her smile. Even if it means going back to school without Deana as a roommate. I certainly didn't think after the year we had that'd be something I'd miss.

But it takes two to mess up a relationship.

And it seems like out of the two of us, she had more of an idea of what she was doing than I did.

"Sweetie, the GPS said to turn back there—"

"Yeah. And the GPS is wrong. I've been to the country club. I know how to get there."

Who'd have thought that at the age of nineteen, I'd still be sitting in the back seat of Mom's car next to my incredibly annoying younger brother, listening to Mom and Cooper and the robotic GPS voice bicker over directions. Mom should have never gotten Cooper that GPS. He seems to ignore its suggestions on principle. And what phone doesn't have a GPS app anyway?

"Calculating new route. Drive straight one mile. Turn right at 48th Street."

"See?" Cooper takes one hand off of the steering wheel to gesture toward the device he's rendered useless.

"All right," says Mom. She clutches her hands together over her purse on her lap and goes back to staring out the front window.

"Do they serve food on little thimble-sized plates at these places?" Owen looks up from his phone to ask me his stupid question, which I don't answer. "I'll think of you while I devour all-you-can-eat Chinese food."

"Thanks." The tiny chain strap of the small black purse Mom

lent me slides down my shoulder and I pull it back up. I feel the tight fabric of my dress squeeze at me with the movement.

"There's no way Junie will be envious of us tonight, buddy." Cooper likes to make a point of listening to his step-kids' conversations. "This is high class dining. With high class people."

My stomach rumbles and I shift a hand over it to dampen the noise it's making. Actually, I could go for Chinese. I don't even know what the event at the country club is, let alone what kind of food they're serving. Assuming I'm not too nervous to eat.

"Ah! Here we are!" Cooper turns on his blinker and joins the line of shiny cars pulling into the country club parking lot. I peer out the window and see mostly endless, endless perfectly-green grass with flags dotted every few hundred feet. It's not until we get farther up that I see the fairly sizeable clubhouse, which is disguised as a Victorian mansion. *This is more where I pictured Rockford living.*

I unlock the door and am about to slip out when Cooper rolls down his window and tells the valet, "Just dropping off my daughter, thank you."

Because I'm sure it's a common occurrence for people coming to dine at the country club to have their parents take them in a compact sedan. *Sure, Deana. Change my major. Never mind school or a place to live—I wouldn't even have my own car to crash in.*

"Have a nice evening, June!" Mom cranes her neck to say goodbye as I crawl out of the car. "Call us when you need to be picked up."

I have to tug on my skirt to keep it low enough over my thighs as I exit. "Okay. Thank you."

And as they pull away, I'm rewarded with Mom waving sweetly to me like I'm a kindergartener they dropped off at school and Owen slamming his face flat against the car window, making his features appear swollen. I slouch my shoulders and look back and forth, desperate to confirm no one else has seen this.

They're gone. I take a deep breath and step inside. There's a line forming inside the foyer, and it dissipates into a grand entryway, where tables are set up and inhumanly-perfect-wrapped gifts dot several white-clothed tables alongside a table with punch and finger foods. I wonder as I pass the table full of gifts why anyone bothered to wrap anything—it's clear about nine in ten gifts are bottles of wine because what else do you give someone celebrating something at a freaking country club? They probably have every-thing, so you have to get them something they'll consume and need more of.

I'm suddenly very self-conscious that I have no gift. Not that I'd even know who or what the gift was for. I shuffle off to a corner and look around for any familiar faces. I don't recognize anybody. And I feel strangely underdressed. I was right, no one is wearing ball gowns, but none of the women have on the little black dress staple, either. Instead, they wear fabric patterns like something out of a Jackson Pollock painting or have strange dips from pieces missing in fabric that make it seem like the dresses are hanging on by being glued to the skin.

At least I have a new pair of shiny flats to stare at as I try to melt into the wall and the fern here in the corner.

I'm starting to draw curious stares from the people who put down their wine, grab a snack and go into the dining area, so I figure I should probably get a move on. There's no one who appears to be working, no one to check my name off a list Rock-ford probably would have forgotten to add my name to anyway. Could I really just crash this party if I wanted to? From the looks I've been getting, I'm thinking someone's going to report I've done just that.

I straighten my skirt, take a deep breath and step inside the dining room, where I'm rewarded with dull overhead lights and a sea of totally indistinguishable faces. I brace myself for the prospect of casually-not-casually brushing past every table until I see Rockford or Addy when I realize there's only one head that's significantly shorter than the rest there at the edge of the center table. It could be another girl, but I may as well start my search there.

It isn't.

"June!" Addy looks up from doodling with a pencil on her placemat and tosses the pencil down, jumping up to hug my legs. I'm taken completely aback by the sudden love for me.

"Hello, Addy." I pat her shoulders awkwardly.

Addy takes a step back and looks up. "I asked Uncle Ev to invite you! I wanted you to read me a story!"

I look down her table for familiar faces, but the only one I'm rewarded with is Isla's, and her eyes could freeze fire just about now. I drop my eyes and search the area where Addy had been sitting. "Do you have any books?"

"No!" Addy lets go of my legs and steps back. "They wouldn't let me bring any."

I fumble my purse open and pull out my Kindle. "I might be able to get something on here." I've never bought a children's book before, and I'm not even sure the place has free Wi-Fi. Probably not. Does the place have free anything? But I have Project Gutenberg books in there. "How about *Alice in Wonderland*?" Way to pick a book she'll want me to continue reading for weeks to come. I'm definitely going to officially become this girl's nanny.

"Okay!" Addy sits down at her chair like she's all business and pats the empty seat beside her. The one right next to Isla.

I sit down and scoot the chair closer to Addy, feeling Isla's eyes on my back the whole time.

Addy peers over my arm to look at my Kindle. "Where are the pictures?"

"There aren't any with this version."

Addy frowns.

I point to the doodles she's done on the placemat. "Why don't you use your imagination and draw some as I read?"

"Okay!" Addy picks up her pencil and waits for me to start reading.

I'm no more than two sentences in when Isla pipes up. "Do you mind? I thought you were here to *keep her quiet*. Not be disruptive yourself."

I stop mid-sentence and turn to glare at Isla. She's smoothing non-existent fly-aways in her hair and staring at a compact mirror. I search the rest of the table desperately for her brother. For *someone* who might put her in her place. But there are two empty chairs on the other side of Isla, and I don't recognize the people sitting at the rest of the table. The woman at the center—maybe in her fifties or sixties, even despite the too-dark dyed hair—seems to be drawing all of their eyes to her with whatever it is she's talking about.

Addy's chair makes a scraping sound across the hardwood floor as she pushes it back. "Come on, June."

She grabs my hand and I get up to follow. With her placemat and pencil in one hand, she leads me to the wall behind us, where chairs are lined up. We sit behind the older woman who's been getting all the attention, a short distance behind the people at the table.

"I don't *like* her." Addy plops down on a chair and lays the placemat across her lap as she starts to doodle, poking holes through the paper. I wish I had something hard to let her draw on. I shouldn't have left all of my favorite paperbacks at home, even if the space in this purse is limited and I have all three on my Kindle.

My eyes flit back to Isla, who's putting her compact away in a teeny tiny glittering purse. "She's not a fan of story time, I think."

Addy and I exchange a grin, and I pick up the story where I left off.

It's hard not to notice when two towering men brush past us on their way to the empty seats beside Isla, even if they hardly notice us. I keep reading, but my voice falters as I sneak a peek and observe Rockford and Blake. They're both dressed in tuxedos —*tuxedos*—when most of the men are wearing three-piece suits and ties. They exchange a few words with Isla, with Rockford waving at the seats Addy and I vacated, and after a short while her pinched nose faces my direction and she nods.

Rockford turns around. I see a softness pass over his features, like water washing away the hardness of the stone. He takes a step forward.

"And then what?" Addy's pencil has stopped moving, and she's staring up at me.

"Oh, uh—" I scan the Kindle to find my place.

"Everett, there you are. Come here."

I stop reading again and look up. Rockford is halfway to us when the older woman turns around, beckoning him over. My eyes meet Rockford's for a moment, and I swallow. I look down quickly to pretend I'm engrossed in reading.

"Alice—"

"Shh." Addy puts a hand on my arm, and I look at her. She's staring at Rockford and the rest of the table. Now that the woman's stopped speaking to her companions, they're all staring at Rockford standing behind her.

"This here is my son, Everett." The woman, Mrs. Rockford I presume, gestures back at him and stares at each of her companions in turn as if to *really* make sure they're listening. They're listening. "He's getting married soon."

I might have expected to feel a number of things at overhearing that announcement: mild disinterest, or slight curiosity, another piece of gossip to share with Margot as she teases me about seeing fictional jerks brought to life wherever I go. What I don't expect to feel is like someone's kicked me in the stomach and knocked the breath out of my chest. *Ah, hello? Heart, please catch up to my brain.*

The table has come to life with polite clapping and a few exclamations of "congratulations."

"Mother, please." Rockford nods to one side of the table and the other.

I hear Mrs. Rockford's laugh, it's somehow both powerful and fun, the kind of teasing laugh that tempts you to want to be her friend even if you know she'll be running the show. "Am I not supposed to share the news yet?"

Rockford clears his throat. "I haven't even…" He stops. I notice

Isla straightening up in her chair, leaning toward all the commotion.

Mrs. Rockford reaches back and pats Rockford on the chest. "Well, pardon me for being a little over-excited. This has been years in the making." She drops the hand and leans toward the man seated nearest her, ignoring Rockford. "His father and I decided no trust fund until he gets married. To a woman we can trust to help handle his part of the business prospects, you know."

"Ah," says the man, a sly smile on his face. "Something to motivate him to choose wisely?"

"Of course! You can't trust a Rockford to just *anybody*, isn't that right?" The comment causes a chorus of laughter. Mrs. Rockford grabs her champagne glass and holds it up, and everyone else at the table does the same. "A toast on my birthday, to my Everett, to the son brought into my life when I married the love of my life. My poor departed Declan."

Everyone turns to face Rockford, their glasses extended. I feel the weight of their stares, the pressure he must be feeling, even if they're looking up at Rockford and not at me. I pretend to bury my nose in my Kindle.

"To Everett!"

Glasses clink and laughter dissolves into murmurs.

Addy slides off of her chair. "Let's go." She tugs on my hand, and I get up to follow.

CHAPTER TWELVE

*A*ddy finds us a dark hallway with chairs lined alongside the wall and plops down, without explaining why she suddenly felt the need to leave her family. I'm wondering if as her 'nanny' I should go back and make sure we have permission to leave—were her parents among the faces I didn't know?—but I don't think I feel up to facing them. I figure we'll just read a chapter here in the quiet, under the sole overhead lamp in the hallway, and then we can go back. We probably won't even be missed.

I'm a few sentences in before I realize we're in the hallway to the bathroom. Lovely.

"I don't want Uncle Ev to get married." It's the first thing Addy's said since we sat down again. She hasn't even brought her placemat and pencils. She's just staring ahead of her, sitting on her hands and swinging her legs.

I put the Kindle down on my lap. I try to phrase my words right. I feel so out of place. I really have no business speaking to her about this. I haven't even gotten used to the lump in my throat I didn't expect to feel when it was finally made clear as day Rockford was unavailable. *Why should I care?*

"Marriage is a change," I say. "It can be hard to get used to changes."

Addy clutches the edge of her chair. "I hate change."

Get used to it, I find myself thinking. *Change doesn't stop happening when you get older.*

I sigh, at the harshness of my thoughts and the awkwardness of sitting there, in the hallway to a bathroom, with a girl I hardly know. "You know," I say, before I even realize I'm going to speak, "I have trouble with change, too." I swallow, thinking about college and the future and everything. "But sometimes it's not up to us."

"I know." Addy's voice gets quiet and she brushes some hair out of her face. "Mommy and Daddy changed. And Mommy forgot about me."

I find myself wondering why Addy is often with Rockford, or at least why he seems more invested in her than a typical uncle. But then again, I hardly know the Rockfords, and their apparently dramatic life is really none of my business. I settle for grabbing Addy's hand and giving it a squeeze. "I'm sorry." I think of my own dad leaving when I was about Addy's age. "But you know, you're not alone—"

"Addy. June. Why aren't you back at the table with the rest of us?"

A chill runs down my spine at the voice, and I turn to look up at the shadowed figure of Rockford. I gaze from Addy to Rockford and back. I hadn't greeted the man who'd invited me, true, but I'm pretty sure my task is to keep Addy out of the way and quiet. But I can't exactly blame her for leading me away if she wasn't supposed to, not if I'm supposed to be in charge of her. "I thought we'd be less likely to disturb you here," I say, taking the blame.

"'Disturb' me?" Rockford cocks an eyebrow as Addy makes a great show of sighing and getting off her chair.

"Well, I mean, all of you—" I start.

"*All right,* I'll go back." She makes a beeline for the table, where she's left her crayons. I get up to follow.

Rockford blocks my path. "Why didn't you tell me you were here?"

I drop my eyes to the ground. "I didn't know where you were. And then you seemed, uh, busy—"

The corner of Rockford's mouth twitches. "Yes. Well, it's Mother's birthday and she loves to make a spectacle." Rockford backs up a bit to let me through. "Come back to the table."

I know I should, but I look at the table filled with glamorous Mrs. Rockford, even more glamorous Isla, and all these people I don't know, and I'm hit overwhelmingly with the need to escape. "I will," I lie. "I just have to—" I turn back, flailing, and remember the bathrooms.

"June? Are you feeling well?" Rockford actually seems concerned.

I pause, clutching my purse tightly to my abdomen. I have to go to the bathroom and he thinks I'm *sick*? "Yes. Of course, I just—"

"You seem pale."

"I'm not." I have no idea if I am, actually, but I have no idea how he knows, either. My eyes have adjusted, but it's really dark down this corridor.

Rockford has the subtlety of an anvil dropped on my foot. "You're upset."

"What? No." I slide the purse under my arm. I sniffle. Talk about terrible timing. I pop open the clasp on the purse and dig through for a tissue.

"I think you are." Rockford crosses his arms and I freeze, realizing he's staring so intently at my face, I feel like an ant under a magnifying glass. "Your eyes are shining. And I think if you say even one more word, you might cry."

The cause of the throbbing headache I'd written off as an annoyance becomes abundantly clear now: I *am* about to cry. And I don't even know why.

Rockford frowns. "Maybe you shouldn't be here tonight."

Thank you, Captain Obvious. I have to wonder what on earth he thought I could do for him here in the first place.

Rockford looks over his shoulder and then back to me. "If I wasn't certain I'm about to be missed, I'd stay and make sure you were okay." He reaches out and almost puts a hand on my arm, but he makes a fist instead and clutches the hand behind his back. "Do you need a taxi? I can get you one."

I shake my head, dabbing the tissue over my eyes. I try to smile, but I can feel the strain the movement's causing to my face. *Recommendation. Rockfords. Recommendation.* "I'll see you Wednesday?" I ask, like I can't wait for another awkward meeting with this man who appears able to summon tears from my cheeks before I'm even aware of them.

Rockford smiles. "Sure. I'm sorry you're not well—"

"Say goodbye to Addy for me." I turn, my hand already reaching into my purse. Maybe I'm not too late for Chinese dinner.

***

I HAD second thoughts about calling Mom and Cooper to come get me so early. So instead, after spending way too long hiding in the bathroom, I find a bench behind some bushes a good distance away from the country club entryway and take some comfort in *Jane Eyre* on my Kindle. I can't shake the feeling that I've just lived a scene from it, but it feels much better on the page, away from the reality of my own feelings.

You can't have a crush on him. On him *of all people. Why on earth would you care if he's getting married?*

Besides, you can't even figure out your life, let alone invite someone else into it.

I make sure to let Mom know I'm ready just a little early. I don't want to run into anyone in the parking lot.

Based on Mom's expression as I slide in next to her, how badly I've failed is still written all over my tear-streaked face. "How'd it go?" she asks, her smile faltering. "Are you all right?"

I buckle up and shake my head, doing my best to get rid of any dourness in my expression. "Yeah. Just a little under the weather."

Mom sighs and turns on the blinker even though there's no one else in the parking lot for her to signal. "I hope you stayed long enough to make an impression."

If the impression you wanted me to leave is a fly on the wall, then sure. "Sure," I say, not in the mood for a discussion.

Mom smiles at me before turning her attention back to the road. "Good. We'll just tell Cooper they were all leaving early."

Seriously? I might be feeling sick and she cares what Cooper thinks? I'm not even sure why this surprises me. But then again, I'm not sick anyway. Not really. So should I really be judging anyone?

"He was really hoping you'd walk away with an offer for a better internship for the rest of the summer."

… Yes. Yes, I should. I clear my throat. "Most jobs and internships are filled for the summer by now. I'm lucky I got the volunteer position at the library."

"I know." Mom pinches her lips as she makes a turn. "But if you have connections, like at Cooper's office—"

I'm surprised that when I open my mouth, that annoying pain behind the back of my eyes is still there. "Mom, it was just a dinner." No sense in telling her I wasn't even there for most of it. My stomach is growling, though, and I switch on Sirius to cover up the treacherous noise it's making. "Besides," I say, "they invited me *because* they like my work at the library. How would it look if I walked out on them?"

Mom looks pensive. "I thought about that… No, you're right. Maybe this experience will lead to something later in the summer."

I was thinking more like something later in my *life*, but I let it go. Still, I guess I'm stuck. There's no way I can just avoid Rockford at the library from now on. I'm just not in the mood to see him when he might mention his engagement or, *shudder*, his wedding plans. Then again, Ms. Fax is sure to go on and on about the most amazing news for the most generous Rockfords, so there's no way

I'm going to avoid it. Not unless I call in sick for the next three or four days.

My phone buzzes and I pull it out, expecting a text from Margot and Deana to ask how the disastrous dinner went. Instead I find a text from Rockford: *I feel terrible you had to go so early. I'll see you Wednesday. And if you're still feeling sick, I just might show up at your house with chicken soup.*

Guess the sick excuse isn't going to help me keep avoiding reality forever.

CHAPTER THIRTEEN

*I*f I thought Wednesday would be hell because I had to see Rockford and confront the bizarre confusion that is my feelings, I would have never imagined how much worse Monday and Tuesday could be. By the time Wednesday afternoon rolled around, I'd had it up to my eyeballs with Ms. Fax's giddy excitement over Rockford's engagement—to one Miss Isla Blane.

Wow, that was surprising. Or not. But it felt kind of like a kick in the stomach the first time I had it officially confirmed. But by now, considering Ms. Fax has managed to somehow work the news into every sentence she normally just punctuates with "the most generous Rockfords"—things like, "So we'll have enough to redo the carpeting this fall, I think, thanks to the most generous Rockfords—oh, did I tell you Everett's mother promised me an invitation to his wedding? Well, not a formal invitation, of course. Those haven't been mailed out yet. But when I called her office to wish her a happy birthday—"—and so on. *Everyone* in the library knows the news and just rolls their eyes. Sinjin keeps giving me these weird looks whenever I catch his eye after she's done it again, so I try to play it cool. By totally avoiding him.

Not that I'm entirely successful.

"Bye, June." Sinjin shifts a backpack higher up onto his shoulder, and I resist the urge to ask what he's got in there.

I smile as best as I can but make a big show of gathering supplies for the summer reading program. "Bye! Have a good evening!"

I feel like we're playing a game at being just colleagues instead of former sort of flames. I can feel Sinjin stand there an uncomfortably long minute longer—my Spidey sense at work—and he just about says something. "Did you—"

"Oh, how wonderful!" Ms. Fax barges out of her office, her hands clasped together, and shuts down whatever it is Sinjin was about to say. "I have to offer my congratulations!"

I don't even have to look up to know, but I do anyway. Sure enough, Rockford is walking past the scanner, his tablet and a storybook tucked under his arm. He's barely had a chance to glance around before Ms. Fax pounces on him, grabbing his hand in hers and shaking it vigorously. She almost causes him to drop his tablet, but she doesn't seem to notice. Rockford saves the tablet with his other hand and looks up, raising an eyebrow wryly.

I don't even realize I'm biting my lip and staring until Sinjin clears his throat. I immediately turn back to the piles of supplies, not even caring that I'm now taking apart the pile of construction paper I just stacked, organizing it by color even though there was no particular need to.

"Well, that's one way to get her to stop talking about him. Wait for him to show up and get all of the attention." He adjusts his backpack again. "See you tomorrow then."

"Bye! Have a nice evening," I say again, realizing how stupid and dismissive it sounds when I just said the same thing.

"Sure," he mutters, and then he walks away.

I don't know how long I stand there shuffling construction paper, but I hear Wyatt groaning and I look up just as Ms. Fax guides Rockford into the back office, her arm wound through his.

"Everyone!" she calls out, too loudly for a library. "Let's offer Everett our best wishes—"

The corner of Rockford's lip twitches. "Violet, please. There's no need." He lets her arm drop and takes a step forward, placing his tablet on top of my pile of construction paper. I nearly jump. "June, we should get going. I saw there were parents and kids already in the story time room." He slides the pile into the crook of his arm and then puts an arm around my shoulder, nudging me forward.

I can feel my eyes bulge, especially with everyone in the office staring. "Yeah," I say, my voice cracking. I lean forward to grab the plastic bin with the rest of the supplies, trying casually to get out of his reach—I'm surprised to find I'm not upset at his touch, but it's the very last thing I need right now—and shuffle quickly past Rockford and Ms. Fax and out of the room.

How I get through the next hour or so is a complete blur. I can't even look at Rockford in the iron-wrought chair without feeling the need to resist the urge to push my eyes back into their sockets. I focus on the kids and corralling their attention to the books.

Even though I can't help but notice more than one mom gazing far too intently at Rockford as he reads. As if he's even that handsome! He's nothing like Sinjin anyway. My eyes flick to Rockford as he turns a page and I can't help but notice how flattering the angle is for that harsh, straight nose.

I immediately go back to organizing construction paper into piles on the crafts table.

Rockford looks so at home on the iron-wrought chair, with the backdrop of the moors behind him. I glance out of the corner of my eye at him from time to time but busy myself with collecting the art supplies, and I see him staring at the wall, as if he can actually see wind rustling throughout the grasses and swamps. I'm acutely aware that it's the first time we've been alone since story time started. I want to slip out without saying anything, but I remember the whole point of this experience, the only reason this man is supposed to be worth bothering about. *'Bearable,' remember? Engaged? Stop pretending he means anything more than a recommendation.*

I tighten the caps on the jars of glitter and place them in the plastic bin on the iron-wrought table beside Rockford. "Addy couldn't make it today?"

Rockford is slow to respond, and when he lifts his head, I'm not at all sure he even heard me. "No." It's not said rudely, but it's not said engagingly, either. He goes back to morosely staring at the wall.

I walk back to the kiddy table to collect the construction paper and lay it beside the jars of glitter in the plastic bin, doing my best not to sprinkle glitter leftovers all over the carpet. Looks like I'll be vacuuming before I leave. "It's an incredible painting," I say, feeling every second of uncomfortable silence. "I don't remember it being here when I was a kid."

"No, it's less than ten years old." Rockford tears his eyes away to meet mine briefly. "Kaitlyn—Addy's mother—painted it. We used to do the summer reading program together."

"Oh!" I nod, stopping the cleanup to examine the wall. "She's talented. Addy likes to draw, too. Does it run in the family?"

Rockford turns away from the wall and stands, suddenly seeming to realize that I've been cleaning up by myself. Not that I pegged him for the type to help anyway. "Maybe." He brushes some sparkles off of his lap and starts collecting the scissors and glue sticks.

"I just thought…" I point to the kiddy table and the arts and crafts supplies in Rockford's hands. "You seem keen to add art activities to every story time."

"That was Kaitlyn's idea." He crosses back to the iron-wrought table and drops the supplies inside the bin. "I'm not artistic. But I'm not really a Rockford."

Okay. That gets my attention. I'm wondering if I should apologize, grab the plastic bin and make my escape, but if I'm going to use him for connections, I can't just leave this conversation dangling. *Would Mom and Cooper tell me to forget this whole thing if Rockford isn't really a Rockford?* "What do you mean?" *I've been calling you 'Rockford' in my head for weeks.*

Rockford collapses into the iron-wrought chair with a sigh and runs a hand through his hair. "My dad married Kathleen—that's Kaitlyn's mother, the one whose party I asked you to attend—when I was fifteen. He was a *plumber* of all things. A plumber called on to do some work for Kathleen, who wasn't even a widow the first few, uh, dozen times she had a leaky pipe or something." He clears his throat. "Although her ancient husband, the true original Rockford, did die after a few years. My own parents divorced when I was young, and I haven't seen my real mother in ages."

"Oh." *Yeah. The family drama.* I hold my hands behind my back for lack of anything better to do. "But does that make you less of a Rockford?"

"It does if you understand these people." When he says 'these people,' he waves a hand around to no one in particular. "Kathleen did adopt me. Although she certainly wouldn't have adopted me even one month later."

I slip onto one of the pillows for the kids, wondering if the gesture will make it seem too much like I'm eager for story time. I just need to end this conversation smoothly and be on my way. But then why do I feel glued to the pillow? "This probably isn't my business. Don't feel you have to—"

Rockford clasps his hands together and leans forward, his arms over his thighs. He smiles. "You're right. It really isn't your business, but I tend to find myself spilling too many secrets when I'm with you, June." He sighs. "Kaitlyn was my age, and… We fell in love."

"With your sister?"

"Step-sister. No, I suppose with the adoption, you're right. My sister." His smile is lopsided. "It was chaste enough. We were in high school."

Apparently you haven't met many high schoolers.

"But your mother wasn't happy."

"No." Rockford gets up and plops down on the cushion beside me.

I find myself so close to Rockford, I have to shift slightly to put an inch more between us.

"Kaitlyn was… Well. I've never known another woman like her."

The line is cliché and doesn't tell me much, but by looking at his face, his eyes so drawn to the painting of the moors, I can't help but feel he might be the first man to utter those words and truly mean it.

"Kaitlyn had a wildness about her, a positive outlook and a love for life I didn't share." Rockford presses his lips together. "Dad and I struggled for years after my real mother left. I was left to take care of myself most of the time, at an age younger than most would be.

"My dad died when I was sixteen." Rockford lets out something like an exasperated laugh, although I don't see the humor. "Kathleen probably adopted me out of some feeling of guilt or nostalgia for the blue collar worker she snatched up as a joke. I don't know. But I was in an even darker place then than I ever was."

"I'm… sorry." I don't know what else to say. My dad has been out of my life for years, but it's not like he's dead. It's not like he was the only family I had.

"Kaitlyn was the only one who supported me. Everyone else— well, they were Kathleen's friends, from the Rockford world. She'd only known my dad a few years, but people acted like she was the one who was suffering the most, not the son he'd left with strangers."

I hug my knees to my chest. Somewhere, at some point, we crossed the line between casual professional relationship and… whatever this is. I don't know if that 'line' was ever properly in place to begin with. I'm not sure how to get us back there, not when some sick part of me is eager to find out more. Not when I feel that flush on my cheeks I don't feel outside of reading my favorite novels. "Kaitlyn's positivity must have been a lifesaver."

"It was. Almost literally." Rockford stretches his legs out and leans back farther into the big pillow. "Back then, I... Well, it was wrong. It was too much."

"Too much?"

"I loved her too much." Rockford sinks entirely into the pillow now, bringing his hands together across his chest. He looks like he might be resting eternally, except that his eyes remain open, his gaze locked on the mural's clouds on the ceiling.

I can't help myself. I'm about to sink down with him to lie on the pillow beside him.

"'I cannot live without my life. I cannot live without my soul.'"

I freeze, shifting my weight onto my forearm. "What?"

Rockford's eyes fall from the ceiling and meet mine. He tries to smile, but he does a poor job. "It's from—"

"—*Wuthering Heights*, I know." I finish sinking into the pillow and stare up at the clouds, too. "I just didn't think you... Well, it's one of my favorite books."

I don't know if Rockford's looking at me. My eyes are locked on the clouds. Kaitlyn somehow painted something and nothing all at once, the clouds masquerading as puffs of smoke when they seem to say so much more.

"It was Kaitlyn's, for a time." Rockford says nothing about me or the fact that he and I both share a passion for this book. Instead, he brings up Kaitlyn, a woman I didn't even know existed until a few moments ago. Where's all the love for Isla? "Her mother didn't approve of her reading 'garbage,' so she was stuck with the classics. She was reading *Wuthering Heights* that summer my dad died, the summer she painted this."

He says nothing for a time, and I know I should excuse myself. But I don't. Instead I bite my lip. "I love *Wuthering Heights*. But it's wrong to think of it as some romantic classic. Of all my favorite books, it portrays the least healthy relationship." Look at that. Am I actually stepping outside of my fantasy world for a minute?

Rockford isn't bothered. "It does when you read it with a mature brain." He pauses. "Well. You're fairly young and still smart enough to see that. But that summer, I was lost. It seemed romantic to me. Hearing Kaitlyn read it made it seem like the most romantic thing ever written." It's so quiet in this part of the library, I can hear him swallow. "A love across classes. A love between two practically-siblings. I don't know what I was thinking—I *wasn't* thinking—but I imagined myself Heathcliff, angry and bitter and full of passion for the only one who ever cared: for Kaitlyn, my Catherine."

"Well, you certainly got the 'angry and bitter' part down even now."

Rockford laughs. "That's right. Heathcliff is worse than ever years after he's lost Catherine. Maybe that *is* part of the reason for my sunny disposition."

I'm surprised Rockford's able to poke fun at himself. No Byronic hero would see the humor in his own suffering. I chew the inside of my lip for a while. I should stop, I really should. Repulsion, curiosity and something like hurt are swirling inside me all at once. "Where's Kaitlyn now?"

"Not dead, if you're looking for parallels between me and *Wuthering Heights*." I'm afraid he'll read my mind and discover just how not far off the mark he is with that statement. "But she did find her own 'Linton.' She did 'straighten up' and date a man her mother approved of. She fancied herself in love with him even while still insisting she felt a passion for me no other boyfriend, no fiancé, no husband could ever match."

Yikes. "All that's left for you is to marry that man's sister. And treat her like crap because you don't really love her."

"That's exactly what my mother seems to have in mind. Well. Minus the 'treat her like crap' part, I'm sure."

I shoot up and lean on my elbow, looking down at Rockford. He seems curious, confused by my sudden movement. "Blake is Addy's father?!"

Rockford sits up, towering over me once more. "You're perceptive. I don't remember saying I was going to marry Isla."

I straighten up myself, but I'm still nowhere near as tall as him, even sitting down. "Please. Ms. Fax wouldn't shut up about your marriage to Isla Blane. But I thought Blake… "

"You thought Blake…?"

I shake my head. "Never mind." I stand up and brush a few sparkles that must have been on the pillows off of my pants.

"You thought he was gay." Rockford stands as well. "He is. He just wasn't… entirely sure at the time, I guess."

"It's really none of my business." I walk over to the container on the iron-wrought table. "Should we get the vacuum, or do you think Ms. Fax would be okay with waiting for the janitorial—"

"June, please." Rockford appears beside me, placing a firm hand atop the container so I can't lift it up. "I kind of make it your business. I can't help myself around you. I just feel like you're the only one I can talk to… "

I have no idea what to say. I pinch my lips and put some space between us. "I guess you don't hate Kaitlyn's Linton." It seems an awfully stupid thing to say just then.

The corner of Rockford's mouth upturns slightly. "I don't curse Kaitlyn to this day for leaving me or consider my soul in the grave for being without her, either."

He's not some fictional jerk from one of your favorite books. And even if he is, you'll never be his Jane, Elizabeth or Catherine.

The thought practically stabs me in the chest.

"Kaitlyn and Catherine still share that bizarre selfishness to this day, though, I must say." Rockford keeps talking, but I'm straightening the pillows, biting back tears. "She left Addy and Blake and is somewhere only God and Mother knows where in Europe. Probably France or England."

Mom wasn't kidding when she said the Rockfords were full of drama. But it was stupid of me to think that was intriguing outside of the written page. I'm so uncomfortable I can hardly clear my throat to speak. I tuck a strand of hair behind my ear and take a deep breath. "It's late. I have to go."

"Oh." Rockford's lips pinch as he picks up the container. "Let's just get this cleaned up then."

"I'm sorry, I'm running late. I have to pick up my brother."

"Okay. But June—"

I'm out of the room, past the information desk to grab my purse from behind the counter, and out the door before I breathe again.

CHAPTER FOURTEEN

*O*wen's right. I have way too many versions of the same story. The same story my brain apparently wants to re-play in real life even when the TV's turned off and the book is closed. The words always dance in front of my eyes, and I'm seeing my favorite books where they aren't, I'm making someone out to be something he isn't.

I'm somehow disturbed that even Rockford sees the correlation between him and one of my favorite books. I haven't been able to stop thinking about it for the past couple of days. The past couple of mind-numbing days at the library, not daring to correct Ms. Fax about her assumptions about an upcoming Rockford marriage—although it's not like he said he *wasn't* going to marry Isla—and terrified Rockford was going to walk through the front door at any second.

I never want to open the books again. I want to focus on something different.

I want to quit the library volunteering.

I open up my texts to read an apology text from Rockford from Wednesday. For being so 'personal.' There's a note about next week's activity.

I decide to compose my resignation letter to Ms. Fax. I have it half formed in my head, despite the part of me screaming that I'm screwed if I do this—but I'm screwed if I don't—when there's a knock on my open door.

"Hey, Spoon! Long time no see!"

I don't know if since breakfast is really "long time no see," but I don't expect Owen to make any sense when he's asking for a favor.

"What do you want?" I ask because I know he isn't in my room to show me how much he misses talking to me.

"You up for some beach volleyball?"

I look at him like he's just asked me to go snowboarding. "Volleyball. At the beach. You do know we don't live in a tropical climate, right? Lake Michigan smells like rotten fish."

Owen shakes his head and plops himself down on my bed, making it shake like he'd tossed a bowling ball onto it instead of just his ass.

"Yes, *volleyball at the beach*. And geez, Spoon, it's 80 degrees outside." You'd think that would be common in summer, but as of late, it's a rarity. "Can my friends and I at least pretend we don't live in an icebox for half the year when it's nice out, or am I supposed to stay shut in with a book like you do year-round?" Owen crosses his arms over his chest. I can see he's ready for his beach bum summer day holiday, since he's wearing his swim trunks and a ratty t-shirt he probably intends to rip off the moment he comes into contact with bikini-clad teenagers.

"Me? Play volleyball? On a beach? You're kidding, right?"

Owen shrugs. "That's what I thought, but I had to ask."

"You had to ask or you needed a ride?"

Owen jumps up and stretches. "Meet you in the car!" And then he's gone.

Yup. Me *taking* him was implied. Whether I wanted to play or not. I get a glance of myself in the mirror on my closet door. Faded t-shirt and yoga pants. Probably not out-of-the-house clothing, but what do I care? Owen isn't wearing much better. Whatever. I grab my purse and stick my Kindle in it. I can swear off the classics, but that doesn't mean I have to swear off reading.

I check with Mom to make sure we have permission to take her car this time. Maybe she'll tell us to stay home. Or offer to take him herself.

No such luck. Her replacement chauffeur is home for the summer. I'm wondering now if we never got yelled at for the party because she's glad she at least didn't have to take him. "Of course! Have fun!"

"Fun" and "chauffeuring my little brother around town" aren't exactly two phrases I'd put together.

"Oh, god, come on!"

"Owen, continuously moaning isn't going to make the traffic move any faster." Although I *am* wondering why the tiny beach-front area is suddenly overrun with cars trying to get a meager parking space just because the sun is out. And then I hear the booming base and the echo of warbling through a microphone and I figure out Owen and his friends have chosen one of those local musical festival days to have their pretend-they're-living-in-Miami beach day.

"Never mind. I'll get out here. I can *walk* faster." Owen opens the door.

"Text me when you're done," I start to say, but he's already shut the door and is on his way.

And I'm stuck in front of and behind cars clamoring for good-old local rock and roll bands like they're actually the Beatles. *Guess I may as well park and enjoy the fresh air,* I tell myself as I'm corralled into an impromptu parking area that's actually just a field of grass. *I've already dragged Mom's car up the curb and through the mud because these parking attendants assumed I wanted in here.*

I get out of the car and grab my purse, thankful I tucked a pair of sunglasses in there before heading out the door. Now to find a shady tree—preferably not downwind of the rock concert. I follow the crowd and cross the street, veering off in the opposite direction when they head toward the cement circular overhang that the town uses for these types of concerts. There are no bleachers, and everyone's carrying blankets and baskets. The miniature picnics dot the hill as far as the eye can see, and I'm so glad I'm headed in the other direction.

I find a nice shady spot that overlooks a small drop to the beach. Kids are playing on the beach—I don't see Owen's group, but I know he must be farther down, from where he originally hoped to be dropped off—but no one's thought to set up their picnic beneath the oak tree but me. I have no blanket, I have no food, but I have my Kindle. Before that, though, I decide to do something. Blame it on the cheery warm air or the blessed sanctuary of the shade. I text Mom that I'm going to look for paying work for the summer to save up. Then, before I can change my mind, I hit send and shove the phone inside my purse, pulling out my Kindle to search for a book.

It's what modern readers like to do, right? Enjoy a breezy, fun contemporary beach read. I didn't think the 'beach' part was literal in the Midwest, but I take it in stride. *Leave the world of the past behind you, June.*

I get to read for all of ten minutes before my phone starts buzzing in my purse. *Got my new job lined up already?* I think to Mom, but that's impossible. It'd take her ten minutes just to compose a text, let alone let Cooper know.

It's from Rockford. And it's a phone call, not a text.

I don't know what I'm thinking, but I answer it. *You were supposed to get a recommendation from him, remember? That means properly saying goodbye to the people you want to leave a good impression on.* "Hello?"

"June! I… I didn't think you'd answer." It's hard to hear Rockford over the buzzy din of the rock concert a distance away, so I plug my other ear with my finger.

"I just thought I should say I'm sorry. I should probably tell you—"

"No, don't apologize." He clears his throat. The music isn't getting dampened at all. I shift around to face the tree, my back to the concert dome, like that will help somehow. "I might have been out of line."

Might *have been?* I purse my lips, thinking about how best to get out of this. There's no way *I'd* give a good recommendation to someone who walked out on me. "I think I might have to quit the library."

The line goes almost silent—except for that annoying music—for an uncomfortably long period. Rockford's the first to speak. "What will you do instead?"

I'm not entirely sure how it's his business, but I may need him as a reference for whatever it is I'm about to do. Even though I have a feeling that will just involve getting crammed into a corner of Cooper's office. "I have to work for my step-dad," I say, not entirely untruthfully.

"That's a shame. But—I'm sorry, it's hard to hear. I'm at an outdoor concert."

I feel like he's reached through the phone and punched me in the chest. The music isn't dampening because it's being fed straight into my ear, the same music. I release my finger from my other ear and sure enough, the same beat, the same warble is echoed a few seconds later in the phone. *Oh shit.*

"June? Can you hear me?"

"Uh, yes, sort of." I jump up and grab my purse, almost running off without my Kindle. My foot kicks it and it skids down the cliff, all the way to the sand below. *Oh, shit.*

I glance around me. There are a lot of people, but I don't see Rockford. I mean, look at the endless blankets—he's probably way in the back. There's no need to panic. *Still no reason not to hurry and get the hell out of here.* I start jog-walking along the side of the cliff, looking for the nearest stairway to take me down to the beach.

"Is that—June, are you at the beachfront concert, too?"

"What?" I'm scrambling to keep my balance on the uneven ground. You're probably not supposed to walk this close to the cliff. *Priorities, June. Is risking death or at minimum broken bones worth potentially avoiding contact with this guy?* I almost tumble, but I keep going. *Apparently.*

Rockford keeps talking. "I can hear the same music coming from the phone."

Uh, is there something else I can blame? Some electronic echo or malfunction? Maybe I'll just play ignorant. The stairs. I scramble along the cliffside, my hand reaching for the handrail. "I can't hear —" I take my first step and Rockford is standing there, his back to me, facing the water. I know it's him. I don't even need to see the phone to his ear to know.

"June?" I hear my name twice, from the man below me and in my ear.

He hears it too. He turns around. His arm lowers slowly, removing the phone from his ear. I'm taller than him for once, standing on the stairs above him. Our eyes meet, and I look away, noticing the grin fading from his lips as I do. He slides his phone into his pocket. "This is a coincidence."

I was thinking more like a cosmic joke, but okay.

I end the call on my phone and slide it into my purse, grabbing hold of one of the handrails. I try to smile. I really do. "Where's Addy?" It's a dumb question, but I don't know what else to ask him.

Rockford gestures toward the hill behind me. "With Blake and Isla. At the concert."

A dog barks from the beach and Rockford turns. I use the opportunity to climb down the stairs and slide past Rockford onto the beach. Captain runs up to Rockford and Rockford bends to pet him, clipping a leash I didn't notice in his hand onto the dog's collar. "I dropped my—" My voice is barely audible. I know I'm mumbling. I need to get what I came for and leave.

I sink my sneakers into the sand, willing myself not to tumble on the warm, uneven surface.

"June." I hear Captain kicking up the sand behind me and Rockford catches up. "It's… It's a beautiful day, isn't it? It's been awfully cool lately."

"Yeah." I'm still a short distance from where I dropped the Kindle. This corner of the beach is strangely deserted, the concert probably drawing everyone over.

He's right next to me now. "When do you start the new job?"

"I… It's not settled yet."

"I can give you a recommendation—"

I stop and try to smile, but I can't look up to meet his eyes. Having him so readily want to dismiss me hurts more than it ought to. The sun is bright, and I feel my eyes water as I cup a hand over them. I didn't put my sunglasses back on when I left the sanctuary of the shade. "I don't need one now, thank you. But I may in a few years."

"When you graduate?"

I nod. I make a point of looking for my Kindle. "I dropped—" I walk away again. If I'm serious about needing his recommendation in three years, I'm probably not doing the best job.

"What type of work are you looking for? I mean, after graduation?"

"I don't know." I peer through the sand. It's somewhere around here. I find the Kindle and pick it up, shaking it free of sand. With my luck, it's probably broken. "Something in business."

"That's rather broad." Rockford is examining the Kindle in my hands and chooses not to comment on what it's doing in the sand, although I can tell he's dying to know. "But that's your major, and that's what you're going to do."

The e-reader still works, although I wonder how I'll ever get some of the grains of sand out of the cracks. "If I must." I slide it into my purse, aching for the comfort of one of my paperbacks. Even if I did swear them off for the foreseeable future. "But I've got three years yet. Three long, long years."

"June, come sit with me." Rockford walks toward a large stone and sits on top of it. He scans the beach—maybe for witnesses—

and unclasps the leash on Captain's collar again, laying the leash beside him on the rock. I don't want to point out it's illegal to have Captain running on the beach without a leash. I don't want an excuse to keep talking, even if I know I should. I sigh. I can't very well ignore him and go if I want a recommendation. I cave and sit down, plopping my purse beside me on the rock. The trees above us, the same ones I sat beneath while reading, offer us shelter from the sun.

Rockford opens his mouth, hesitates, and then puts his foot into it. "I'm worried about you."

It's not at all what I was expecting or hoping. I feel like I've sat down for a lecture from Cooper. "What are you talking about?"

"You're young yet, I know." Rockford squints and looks out toward the beach, where Captain is splashing along the coast line. "But I feel like in a lot of ways you're mature, too."

How little you actually know me. "Thanks. I suppose."

Rockford turns and examines me. I have to look away. "You don't seem to like majoring in business."

"I don't." Wow, that's going to win me points with Mom and Cooper. *You're admitting it to the one person they were hoping would get you a job in said field.* "It doesn't appeal to me."

"What does?" He waits for me to answer, but I have nothing to say. He points to my purse, where I've stored my Kindle. "Books? Reading?"

"Sure, but—"

"So why not consider being a writer? Or a full-time librarian? Even a teacher—"

"Thanks, but I know all the possibilities. And none are appealing to my parents."

"Ah." Rockford nods. "You mentioned one time that not everyone is free to choose a career that's their passion. June, my dad was a plumber—"

"I know." I squeeze the fingers on my left hand with my right. "I understand the mindset of being practical. I understand what my parents want from me."

"But that doesn't mean you have to sacrifice your passions."

"I don't have a passion I'm sacrificing." I fling my hands up off my lap slightly, just short of flinging them wildly in the air. "I don't *know* what I want to do, just that I need to do *something*." I pinch my lips. "It's not like I'm stifling this passion to be a writer or that I could see myself teaching children—"

"Addy thinks you're *great* with kids."

"She has more faith in me than I do." I feel my lips curling into a smile. "I don't even think… If Mom and Cooper said they'd support whatever I chose to do, I couldn't pick something."

Rockford nods and stares at his hands, which he's clasped together over his knees. "I probably would have said the same at your age. But my future was already written for me."

"Your mother wanted you to work with her, even after everything with you and Kaitlyn?"

Rockford grimaces. "Kaitlyn was married by then. Young, I know. But Mother thought it would be the end of it all. That we'd all just pretend it never happened, just like she did." He looks up. "But I shouldn't have let her decide for me. I know that now. I'm just… warning you not to do the same."

"I'll miss the library," I say, the words out before I can think them. "The whole reason I volunteered was to avoid working at my step-dad's office. To do something meaningful, even if it was only meaningful to me."

Rockford surprises me by laying a hand over mine on my lap. "It was meaningful to me." His smile falters slightly. "Even if it was only for a short while."

I let his hand linger for just a moment, and then I pull it away, casually, I hope. "I'm glad. I'll miss story time." I try to bite my tongue. I try to stop it. "I'll miss you." I don't even realize it's true until I say it. But it's true. It's stupid. I can't help but remember how he acted, but all I can think about is his engagement, Cooper's office and endless school ahead of me, ripping me further and further from the library and the painting of the moors and the few short weeks I spent planning story times with him.

Rockford removes his hand from my thigh slowly, almost reluctantly. At first I'm sure I've said the wrong thing. He takes a deep breath. "We've become fairly good friends considering the short amount of time we've known each other, don't you think?"

Friends. I'm not even sure it accurately describes our relationship. He spent half the time belittling me, I spent half the time avoiding him. What are we? A mess. "Yes." It's better than the truth: that we're nothing to each other, not really. A blip on the overall timeline of our very different lives.

"In some cultures," Rockford says, showing off his little finger, "people meant to have some impact on one another are tied together by an invisible red string." He shakes his pinky toward my hand. "Sometimes I feel like you and I are tied."

"And that if one of us were to leave, the cord would snap, and I should take to bleeding inwardly."

"What?" Rockford is smiling, curious.

"It's from *Jane Eyre.* Sort of." I hold my hand out, extending my pinky. "Although I suppose it makes more sense there, where Rochester thinks the cord of communion is tied to the heart."

Rockford touches his pinky to mine briefly and then pulls back his hand, grinning. "And you say you have no passions."

"None that can translate to practical use."

"Perhaps you just don't know how they can yet."

"Perhaps."

We both look away, staring out at the lake and the way Captain kicks up little waves of water as he moves back and forth.

Rockford's the first to speak again. "I don't think you'll miss me as much as I'll miss you."

The words seem so surreal, so clichéd yet never more meaningful, and they're almost drowned out beneath the sounds of the barking and the waves, so I'm not too sure I'm hearing them. "I'm not the one getting married." It seems a petty thing to say. Too obvious, too.

Rockford's head turns. His eyes, dark and searching, pour over my face. "I'm not getting married."

"But Isla—"

"Isla fancies herself my fiancée because my mother said she'd make a good pick." He snorts and shakes his head. "Mother already vetted the family when choosing a groom for Kaitlyn. Why bother going through all that again when there's a young single woman available?"

"But you—" I bite my lip. "You didn't show for the first story time to spend time with her."

Rockford laughs bitterly. "That wasn't what happened. But she did show up at my place uninvited when I finally got home from dealing with some work emergencies."

"Oh."

"Not even Blake wants me to marry Isla. Not even Addy, and Isla's already her aunt anyway, so there's no escaping her." He squeezes my hand. "I can't marry her, or anyone else. I've fallen in love with you."

I forget how to breathe. I stand up, releasing my hand from his, panicking, not even sure what I'm panicking about—his confession or his lie? Why didn't he tell me earlier? "Don't play with me! We hardly know each other. I'm nothing compared to you— middle class, confused, untalented." I shake my head to stop him from speaking. "No, I know that. But it doesn't mean that I'm not a human being, that I don't have feelings of my own, jumbled as they may be. I'm not some pointless summer flirtation! Some little game to pass the time before you decide you'd better marry for your trust fund anyway."

Holy crap. I'm living a scene out of Jane Eyre.

"June, I don't think of you that way—"

"But you *do!*" I cross my arms and focus on stopping the tears from falling. I can't help it. Sense of déjà vu or no, this is happening. And my favorite fictional love interests aren't making for a great love interest in real life. "And even I know a beauty like Isla is better suited for one of the Rockfords."

Rockford stands and something flashes across his face I can't read. Sadness maybe. "Come off it, June!" Rockford clenches his fists to his side. "Isla is nothing to me. She's vain and snobbish and boring." He takes a few giant steps, closing the distance between us before I can even think to stop him. He places his hands on the sides of my arms. "You. I can't stop thinking about *you*. You, middle class and confused—and maybe not knowing her talents just yet."

"You can't be serious." But I *am*.

"You don't believe me." I watch his face. Though it's never terribly expressive, although I've only rarely seen him look happy, there's something more to the graveness of his face now. Something like a light fading from his eyes.

My heart is beating three times too fast. He looks like Rochester, Darcy or Heathcliff, torn away from their lovers—and I'm melting. "I do." I wrap my arms around him, stand on my toes, and meet him halfway for a kiss.

For a few precious seconds, my mind shuts down. I don't think about the future. I don't think about stories from the past. I don't even think about the absurdity of being caught up in this moment. I'm just here, feeling his lips on mine, living the warmth that travels up from the tepid sand through my legs all the way to the top of my head.

My heart knows something my brain refused to let me know. Even now, as I put my hand on his chest and softly push him away, my mind is screaming why this won't work out, why this is nuts. Pushing, pushing the feelings away.

"I'm sorry," I say, and I find myself breathless. "I think we might be moving too fast."

His grin is lopsided. "One kiss is too fast?"

Since I haven't been kissed in well over a year, it is for me. I pat his chest. I'm not sure why. My hands are shaking, my heart looking for some reason not to let go. My phone buzzes from over by the rock, and I shimmy out of Rockford's arms to go get it.

"June—"

I slip the phone out. It's Owen, actually bothering to tell me Sinjin is giving him a ride home in a car he must have borrowed from his parents. Or "sj's hooking me up for ride see ya," which is close enough. "I need to go."

"Is it something bad?"

"No." I shake my head and turn. Rockford's stepped beside me, and I do my best to soften his concern with a confident smile. "I just… My brother… "

"Always you and your brother." He raises an eyebrow. "I'll come with."

"No!" I drop the phone into my purse and slide it over my shoulder. I can't look at him. "No. I mean, thank you, but—" I bite my lip. "Call me." I try to seem more confident than I am as I meet his eyes.

"Okay." Rockford's studying me, and I'm afraid he's reading my mind and the strange, conflicted thoughts that are burrowing themselves in there. Captain chooses this moment to run up to Rockford, nudging his hand with his nose. Rockford pets him absently and I'm gone, back the way to the stairs and the cliff and the annoying mumbled concert.

"June, I can walk you—"

But I'm out of hearing range. At least that's my excuse. The walk between the beach and my car is a blur, even with the people milling about between here and the lake.

I get into the car and take a moment to rest my arms atop the steering wheel, burying my forehead beneath them.

In Jane Eyre, *Jane agreed to marry Rochester after his confession.* I take a deep breath. *But this isn't a book. And you're not a heroine.*

… But he still wanted you.

I get out of the car and make my way back to the beach.

CHAPTER FIFTEEN

It's my first week at Cooper's office. I don't even know why I'm avoiding the library anymore. I feel like the decision had already been made for me—I'd already told Mom and Cooper I was done for the summer, that I needed to earn money. I'd already gotten their hopes up. How could I say no when Cooper told me he'd gotten me a job that very evening? *It's just for the summer. It's not forever.*

But whenever I do settle on a career, it'll probably be something just as bad. And that *will* be forever. I groan inwardly every time I remind myself of that.

"I'm going to the library," I tell Mom after dinner. "Can I borrow the car?"

"The library?" Mom looks at the wall calendar hanging up next to the fridge. "Ah. Wednesday." She digs her keys out of her purse. "You know, even working at Cooper's office, you might still find time to help with that story time program." She might be winking. She's either slyer than I pictured her being, or she's happy because she thinks my 'purely professional' relationship with Rockford is still something that'll score me some good-earning job in another three years.

"Thanks," I say, grabbing the keys. I look at the clock. It's actually too late for story time, damn the 8-to-5 shift at Cooper's office. But Rockford texted me afterward that he might be back later and I have a sudden, ceaseless urge to see the moor on the wall.

What I don't expect when I walk into the library is for half of the library staff to come over and ask me what I've been up to.

"Working," I answer. Now that I have no one to avoid, I *really* wish I hadn't told Mom I wanted to quit. They miss me after three days. I've never felt so wanted.

Gracia updates me on her nephew's graduation party and the next addition to the library—some machine to repair books donated by the Rockfords, naturally—and then gets called away when a patron stands by the information counter. "Good to see you!"

You'd think I'd been gone three months instead of three days.

From the pinched expression on Ms. Fax's face as she glowers over at me from behind the counter, I'm guessing *she* wishes it'd been three months before I showed my face here. Thank god I'm not aiming for her recommendation—although if I think about it, it'd make more sense. But it wouldn't be pretty.

I step into the story time room to get away from her beady eyes, and there's a mom and two kids by the bins near the entryway. I pretend I'm looking for something in particular and start browsing through the bins closer to the story time corner.

"June." The voice is hushed, whispered.

I look up, half expecting to see no one, just my name echoing across the fictional moors—but I find Sinjin, curled up on the big pillows the kids sit on with one of the laptops you can check out from the library.

"Sinjin," I reply, and my heart sinks. There *is* someone I should have thought to avoid at the library… In the strange euphoria of the past half a week, I almost forgot all about him. I sit on the cushion beside him. "You're volunteering this late?"

Sinjin shrugs. "I finished a while ago, but I just wanted to do some work where it's quiet."

I cock my head. "Quiet? In the children's story time room?"

Sinjin looks around. "It's getting late. Kids are going home."

I chew the inside of my lip, wondering if I should text Rockford to ask if he's really coming back or if we should meet somewhere else. My thoughts are so lost on Rockford, it takes me by surprise when Sinjin speaks again. "Did you know Deana applied for the full-time page position opening this fall?"

It takes me a little while to respond. "Yeah." I move a loose lock of hair behind my ear. "I told her about it."

Sinjin shifts the laptop off his lap and onto the floor. "How come you didn't apply?"

I'm not sure how he knows this, but it's true. "I'm going back to school."

Sinjin nods, gathering his knees in his arms and hugging them against his chest. "If you were going back for something you could stand, I'd understand, but—" He stops when he sees me staring at him. "What?" He grins. "You've become quite the topic of discussion when I check in with my sisters."

"Nothing like asking some people in France about the girl next door." I smirk.

"Oh, I've gotten plenty of France stories, too." He nudges my arm with his. "But you're more interesting to talk about."

"If you say so." I'm probably not going to get far if I argue. Even if he's totally wrong. I look at Sinjin, really *look* at him, for the first time in forever. I've been so eager to avoid remembering that he was a part of my past—that he could be a part of my future— that I've been treating him like he's not even a person. Like he's not even my friend. Just a big ball of hotness that I can't bear to look at because I get so flustered. But I'm *not* flustered now. "Sinjin, I—" I don't know what I want to say. I might be imagining things. We weren't even that serious.

Sinjin must be reading my mind. "What you and I had in high school. I didn't take it seriously enough. I was a little embarrassed." Sinjin sighs. "I'm too young for you, I know. At least for the next couple years."

"It's not that you're too young—" *Although that's part of it.*

"But who knows where life will take us in the next few years?" Sinjin stands and extends a hand down to me. I hesitate, but I take it and let him pull me up. I have the briefest of flashes, remembering how he took my hand before slipping his arms around my waist as we slow danced. "Besides," he says as he tries to smile, but he sort of stumbles, "Margot and Deana told me: you're dating Everett Rockford."

Well, that was news to me. I guess I wasn't vague enough when I last texted them. I let my hand fall from Sinjin's and dig my phone out of my purse, scrolling through my recent texts.

"What is it?" Sinjin asks. He sounds concerned. I realize I've left him hanging.

"Nothing. It's just… I didn't tell Margot or Deana I was dating Rockford. Explicitly anyway." I see a text from Margot: *JUNE YOU NEED TO CONTACT ME NOW!!* It's the third such text. But I'm waiting for a text from Rockford. I meet Sinjin's eye and notice the eagerness in his expression. "I guess I might be." Something dark flashes over his eyes, and I take his hand in mine and squeeze. "But I know at least that you'll always be special to me. You were probably my first love." I feel incredibly bold and incredibly stupid to admit as much out loud. I'm not even sure what's come over me.

Sinjin squeezes my hand back and looks away. "Then I came to realize the same thing too late."

My heart breaks and for the briefest of seconds I want to hug him like I did in high school. I want to melt right back into the life with fewer responsibilities, without that dreaded cloud of 'the future' hanging over my head. But I feel like that time has passed. I may not know where I'm going, but I can accept where I've been— and I can let it go.

My phone buzzes. *Sorry I wasn't able to stay at the library after the reading. Want to come over? I want to talk about story time.*

I feel myself blushing at the images that flashed through my head at the invite before I read the last sentence. It's *way* too soon.

"I should get going," I say, tucking my phone into my purse. "But I hope to see you around."

"Sure." Sinjin slips his hand out from mine. "See you." He slides back onto the cushion on the floor, picks up his laptop and stares at the screen, but his eyes aren't moving, and I'm sure he's not reading. I linger for just a second longer and then go.

I TAKE A DEEP BREATH, readjust my sweater—which might be just a little too short to properly cover the waistband of my jeans, but I was in a hurry after work and the temperature dropped at least ten degrees since the afternoon—and knock on the door.

I totally expect to see Rockford on the other side of it. What I don't expect is for him to be wearing this grin on his face that totally knocks the wind out of me.

I clutch my hand to my mouth to cover a gasp.

"What?" he asks, cocking an eyebrow. "Is there something on my face?"

This feels like the most clichéd exchange in the book. I laugh and let my hand drop. "No. Sorry." He backs up and lets me pass by. I slip my finger into the heel of my shoe to slip it off.

Rockford does this thing where he cradles his arm against his side and rubs his upper arm subconsciously and I just about melt. "You can keep those on if you like."

I flex my toes on the hardwood floor as I drop my purse off on his counter. "I'm more comfortable this way. Unless you'd prefer…" I wonder if I should have worn some socks, but I notice Rockford's not wearing any socks or shoes, either. He somehow looks both as stiff as I half expect him to look and completely relaxed in jeans, a white t-shirt and a light gray sweater.

I realize I'm staring at his feet and clear my throat, snapping back to attention. "So," I say, awkwardly clapping my hands together. "How'd story time go?"

Rockford laughs, but it's more like he finds my awkwardness

adorable than he's found anything I've said funny. His smile suddenly vanishes and he holds up a finger. "Oh, wait—first, I've got something for you."

He trudges down the hallway and I stand there, rocking on my feet, unsure of what to do. It's a bit early in this relationship—this *relationship*? Am I hearing myself correctly?—for gifts, isn't it? Or is it perfectly normal? I think back to the sort-of relationship I had with Sinjin. We just went to dances pretty much, so the most I got from him was a spaghetti dinner and a corsage. Maybe it depends on the gift—

"June?" I hear my name from down the hall. "Are you coming?"

Oh. Right. *Follow* him. I scuttle down the hallway, unsure where to find him.

"In here!"

I stop at a little doorway halfway to the fireplace and step inside. It's a sunroom of sorts, a small addition at the back of the condo with just enough room for a table and a sofa. Even with the sun setting in an hour or so, the effect of sunlight in the room is nearly blinding. It's so bright bouncing off of all of the white, it's hard to believe it's barely 60 out.

I grin as I step inside, overwhelmed by the bright white of the room, from the walls to the rug to the sofa. I try my best to stop myself from shielding my eyes, but I'm probably not seeing clearly, as I practically bump into Rockford beside the doorway.

"Here. I mean, it's nothing special." He's holding a hardcover book in both hands, and he thrusts it at me. "And I just realized you were probably expecting something much better—"

"No! I—" I take the book from him and examine it, cracking it open. *"Wuthering Heights?"*

Rockford runs a hand through his hair. "Hear me out," he says. "This will make more sense in a minute." He sits down on the sofa and grabs his tablet off of the armrest. "I was thinking about how we both liked the book." He taps his screen and then looks up, grimacing just a little. "You almost definitely already *have* it—"

"I do." I run my fingers over the front cover of the book. It's one of those cute editions probably from Barnes & Noble I always sort of wanted—an artsy hardcover printed copy of a public domain classic just *screaming* to be part of a huge home library. The kind I could only justify having in my dreams. I smile and look back at Rockford, and the look on his face almost kills me—it's like I just slapped him. "Oh, but I love this! Thank you! My copy is pretty much falling apart." I sit down on the floor in front of the sofa awkwardly, clutching the book to my chest, not sure how I managed to mess things up in less than five minutes.

Rockford doesn't comment on my odd seating choice and instead slides off the couch to sit down next to me. "Good," he says. "I'm sorry it's such a lame gift—"

"*Stop!*" I say, nudging his shoulder with mine. "It's perfect. Really." I massage my finger with the textured cover again. "It's almost like you already know me. I mean, like *really* know me."

I can't look at Rockford for long because I can practically feel the invisible string between us, threatening to pull his face closer to mine. I just about die thinking about our first kiss the other day, and I quickly turn my attention to the tablet on his lap. "What's that?" I ask, the words 'story time' the only things I can clearly make out.

"Oh, right." He taps the screen and rotates it, so I have a better view. "So, you know the whole inspiration for the mural was *Wuthering Heights*, more or less."

I grimace, thinking how the whole inspiration for his relationship with his sort of sister/sort of ex was one of my favorite novels. "Right," I say, at last, my throat dry. I'm scanning the document and it says "19th century living," followed by a number of bullet points. "And it was set in the mid-19th century…?" I wait for him to explain the connection.

"Yeah," says Rockford, taking his tablet back. His fingers graze the back of my hand as he does, and I'm overwhelmed with the same type of thrill I get in seeing characters like Jane and Rochester or Elizabeth and Darcy just barely touch. "And I know talking about classic romantic literature will just about bore the kids to pieces."

I laugh, picturing Addy forced to listen to a book with no pictures about people courting one another in a time when passion was pretty slow to build. At least maybe she'd like the dog, Pilot, who appears in *Jane Eyre*. If she could make it that far.

Rockford continues unabated. "But why not tell kids what it was like to be a kid in that era in England? To tie things in with the mural? Kids ask about it all the time."

I'm thinking of *Jane Eyre* and how she grows up abused, alone and unhappy, or how Catherine and Heathcliff start their rather strange obsession with one another at probably too young an age. Maybe the Bennets several decades earlier might be a better example of a good childhood, if you could get past the ever-bickering parents and chaos of a household with five children.

"That could be fun." I shimmy my butt around and lie back on the floor, using the couch as a footstool. "Do you want me to consult Ms. Brontë for descriptions of life for children?" I thumb open my new book and turn through the pages looking for passages. They're practically on the tip of my tongue, and I feel like I should know where to find them, but I have to adjust to the new wrappings in which I find my favorite words.

My eyes flick past the book for a second and I find Rockford staring at me, his eyebrows raised and his mouth agape just a fraction.

"What?" My gaze flicks guiltily to my feet. On his pristine white sofa. I pull them back. "Sorry! I was just getting comfortable to read. I didn't even consider where I was—"

"It's fine!" Rockford lifts a hand out to stop me from speaking further and pivots so he lines up next to me. He lies back and puts his own feet up on the cushions. He holds his tablet out just like I held my book. "Seems comfortable to me."

I feel something unclench in my chest and I snuggle back into position, my feet raised. I feel so stupid, but so right at the same time. My elbow is touching Rockford's, my shoulder nestled against his. We both read in silence for what feels like forever. Actually, I'm just re-reading the same sentence over and over, suddenly unsure how to breathe.

My head tilts in toward his, and I find he's already gazing just slightly toward me. Our eyes lock.

"What were we looking for again?" I ask, and I realize I actually have no idea at all.

Rockford puts his tablet on the ground beside him and reaches up for my book. I'm so numb, he encounters a little resistance—I'm clutching onto the book for dear life, like him taking it away is going to leave me without something to keep my hands in check.

"*June*," says Rockford, and it's so quiet, so soft, so *pleading*, I just about lose all the strength in my body. The book slides effortlessly out of my hands and is tossed somewhere on the ground beside Rockford's tablet.

And then his arms are around my back, clutching me closer, somehow squeezing the small gap between us into nothingness so that I'm inhaling the warmth of his breath. On the floor, the difference in height between us is nothing when I'm pulled up to see him face to face.

There's so much hanging in the air between us. I see Rochester's weakness for Jane, Darcy's new experiences with openness and humility with Elizabeth, and even Heathcliff's infatuation with Catherine all in his eyes. My mind races through my imagined versions of each couple proclaiming love and through the film and stage adaptations, but I realize that the 'camera' is off. I'm not an invisible observer, looking in. I'm living it. I'm the heroine. And Rockford is my hero.

The crackling tension in the air between us breaks and Rockford's lips press against mine, gently at first, then harder and harder, without being too much, never quite enough. His hand runs up my back to the back of my head and his fingers wrap through my hair. We come up for air, but it's like we're drowning even when breathing, each excruciating moment apart too long so we never quite fill our lungs. I drink in his mouth, his cheeks, his chin, anything I can—it's more satisfying than oxygen. I grip his back tightly, run my hands up to his shoulders, hook my feet around his calves.

He opens my mouth with his, and we share one breath, his tongue dancing atop mine. He breaks away and runs his kisses over my ears and my neck, prying at my sweater to kiss the skin of my shoulders. I'm so hot—it's so *hot* in here, I should have never worn a sweater in summer—but I'm terrified of taking it off, terrified of how giddy I feel at the idea, afraid I'll lose grip on what I know. It's too soon. I don't know him well enough. This is crazy. I'm not… ready.

I plunge my hands under his sweater, knowing at the very least his t-shirt is there to stop me, but I want to feel his biceps, absorb the moisture pouring off his skin. My leg pulls his body closer, my groin nestles into his abdomen.

"Whoa!" Rockford pulls back from my neck, drinking in an inexhaustible breath of air. His hands tremble now on my arms. "Do you… Are you… Should we?"

He's tentative, sort of grinning. I can tell it's an effort for him to smile, to keep this small but too-great distance between us.

I bring my hands out from under his sweater and collapse back to the ground entirely, falling free from Rockford's shaky embrace to stare at the ceiling. "Maybe not," I say, as a compromise between my brain shouting, "It's too soon! Stop!" and my body yelling, "Hell, yes!" I fan my hand over my face.

I hear Rockford readjust himself beside me. "Yeah, I thought so. I'm sorry… "

I turn to see Rockford lying on his stomach, propping himself up on his elbows. "Don't be," I say, rolling myself over to echo Rockford's position. I bump the top of my forehead softly to his. "I just need more time. I…" I swallow, unable to speak. *I didn't even know we were officially dating.*

Did either of us actually ask the other one out here?

Rockford takes my hand in both of his, keeping his head right against mine. "You don't need to explain yourself." He pulls his head back slightly and smirks. "I really did bring you over here to talk story time."

I smile back. "I believe you." I lean forward and peck him on the cheek. Anything more and we'll be right back where we started. I roll away and pick up my book, holding it up in the air. "You just didn't know that this type of gift makes me weak in the knees."

Rockford raises his eyebrows and rolls over, picking up his tablet. "Note to self," he says, typing something on the screen. "Buy June more books."

I slap the book hard on the ground and tackle him, pinning him beneath me.

orry I was late replying to you! I'm home now. I can chat if you want, but you're probably busy.

I put the phone down on the bed beside me, turn on the TV and settle in for a way-too-late-at-night mind-numbing session before bed. But I can't sleep. My fingers trace my lips. I can't get the taste, the *feeling* of his lips on mine out of my head.

The picture has barely appeared on the TV screen when the phone buzzes: *Turn on video chat now!*

I do. It's early morning in France, and I expected Margot to be busy sleeping or enjoying croissants at a café or something. When her picture appears on the screen, Deana is beside her and they're walking together. I can tell from the way they bob up and down. "June!" The twins say in unison, staring at the screen.

"Margot and Deana!" As long as we're playing the 'yes, I know your name and can shout it' game.

"We messed up." Deana is bouncing up and down on the screen and kind of making me dizzy. "Remember how we both volunteered at the library?"

"Yeah... Are you guys walking somewhere? We can talk later if you want—"

"No, no! This is important!" Margot grabs the phone out of Deana's hand. "Well, the reason we both wanted to volunteer at the library is because we used to go to story time there. Like nine years ago."

"*You* went to story time," interrupts Deana, "I was a little more interested in books appropriate for my age."

"Shut up!" Margot says it playfully, lightly slapping Deana on the chest. "You know I was there because I liked helping out with the little kids, not because I was into the story."

"Wait, wait, wait." I hold a finger up to the screen like that will somehow stop the twins from talking. "You two went to Rockford Private Library as kids? But you just transferred here in high school!"

"We *told* you we'd lived there briefly before, remember?" Deana rolls her eyes.

"Yeah, but just for like half a year—"

"During the summer," says Margot. "Dad was asked to consult for a few months. This was when the story time summer reading program was led by a couple of teens. A brother-sister combo... "

I swallow. "Rockford and Kaitlyn." If I were smart, I wouldn't have blabbed about the two of them to my friends, not when I wound up sort of kind of—almost definitely—dating Rockford shortly after. But I'd no one to vent to after Rockford's weird admission. And fiancée or no fiancée, I couldn't imagine I was on the list of dateable prospects for him. Which reminds me, I really need to get on him for that *'bearable'* comment ...

"Yup." Deana nods. "We even saw them painting that wall design together."

"Okay..." I say. "And by the way, how does *Sinjin* know anything about me and Rockford? Especially since I didn't tell *you* we were dating!"

Margot and Deana stop suddenly in their tracks and exchange a look. "So it's true," Margot says.

I want to put the phone down just so I can cross my arms, but I settle for glaring at them. "Who told you?! I wasn't exactly clear on that myself until recently. We haven't even really discussed it, actually… "

Margot and Deana look at one another again as if mentally sending out waves deciding who's going to break the news. Margot takes a deep breath and takes the plunge. "Kaitlyn."

"Kaitlyn Rockford. In France?"

"Yes!" Deana shifts the phone around and points the camera at a building. It takes a couple of seconds for the image to focus, but I notice it's a café. Not that surprising in France, but this café is so stereotypical, I would have thought the two were walking around in a theater backdrop meant to resemble France. The camera flips back to Margot and Deana. "She owns this café!"

Kaitlyn Rockford left her husband and daughter and even Rockford… to run one more unnecessary café in France?

"Margot recognized her first." Deana nods at her sister. "First we noticed her just for being American—she's got a dreadful accent—but Margot knew she seemed familiar. I thought she was crazy, but—"

"It dawned on me that she was Everett Rockford's sister!"

Deana looks annoyed by Margot's interruption. "Yes. And *anyway*, she came over, and Margot opened her big mouth—"

"Oh, come on, I wasn't expecting it to be a big deal!"

"—about where we were from and how we knew her from the library. She seemed happy that we remembered her at first." Deana takes a few steps, probably realizing she seems strange standing in front of a café and talking into her phone screen. "Then Margot brought up how our brother and friend were volunteering there this summer, how you were working with Everett on the summer story time program—"

Margot peeks her head over Deana's shoulder to pop on screen. She grabs the phone so it focuses on her. "And she like *freaked out*. Like *freak out*-freaked out."

I'm not sure what that means. But I have a sinking feeling in the pit of my stomach that I get the picture.

Deana pulls the phone back. "She wanted to know if you were

the gold digger he just told her he was dating. The one their mother would hate if she found out about you."

"Rockford talked to Kaitlyn?" I ask. *About* me? "He said she left her husband and child and was off somewhere in Europe. I thought he didn't even know where she was."

Deana shakes her head. "Well, he did. Or he does now. They apparently just talked earlier that day, and she was *shaking* over it. And she told us to get out—didn't even want us to pay, just *get out*, and tell *our friend* not to stick her nose where it doesn't belong and leave 'her Ev' alone."

"And you decided to walk back to her café just to… show me?"

Margot and Deana exchange a look. "We were in the neighborhood when I got your text anyway," says Margot. "And—"

A bell jingles. Like the kind that hangs from shop doorways to let people know when someone has left or entered. "Is that *the gold digger* Ev thinks he's dating?"

It was as if written in a romance novel. Maybe an Austen one. Women are gossiping and the wrong person overhears. Because coincidences like that just don't happen in real life. But the twins kind of walked right into that one for me.

I toss my shoulders back and decide to be brave like Elizabeth. "Can I say something to her?"

Both Margot and Deana are looking off screen. And both have suddenly lost a few shades in skin tone. They look like someone caught them in the middle of a crime. "Uh…" Margot clutches the phone to her chest, and I can't see a thing.

"Oh, I have something to say to *you!*" The phone camera shakes and all of a sudden I'm face to face with a beautiful brunette. She has dark eyes covered by thick dark eyebrows arched in such a way, I can feel the scorching hatred seething through the ocean to get to me. She's gorgeous, too, and I'm suddenly well aware I'm in my sweats with my makeup washed off. "Stay away from my brother."

I probably should introduce myself, say something less likely to incite her rage further, but the way she's butting into my business kind of pisses me off. "Excuse me?"

"Stay. Away. From. Everett."

I scoff. "I don't see how that's any of your business. Especially since I've spent more time with your daughter in the past few weeks than you have." Now that I think about, it's strange that if she wants this 'gold digger' away from her family, she doesn't issue an order for me to stay away from the one person she might have any authority over.

She doesn't even respond to that. "Are you dating him?" I can't see her full body, but I can tell from the way her shoulder is angled that she has one hand on her hip.

"No!" I want to lie and say yes—I mean, who makes out with 'just a friend'? Besides Deana. But I haven't even talked about it with Rockford. Why am I discussing this with his flake of a sister?

"Good. He must be delusional as usual." Kaitlyn pinches her lips together. "I want you to give me your word that you never will date him, either."

"What?" I can feel the rage burning inside me, and I hope she's getting some of it long-distance, too. "I will not!"

Kaitlyn's eyes widen. "Excuse me? Do you know what dating someone like *you* would do to him?"

"You don't even know me!"

"I know enough." Kaitlyn takes a deep breath as if she has to or she'll crush Margot's phone in her palm. "If Ev marries anyone but someone Mother would approve of, he'll lose his trust fund."

"That's *his* choice." Why am I defending the idea of him dating me? He's never officially asked me out. I mean, we are basically heading that way, but… "And I don't care about his fortune." Why should I? I can't picture Mom and Cooper being all right with me marrying a rich guy and then relying on him to support me. I'll be working a career they can brag about no matter how much money is in the bank.

Kaitlyn is unmoved. "He'll be shut out by the family."

"I doubt the family who *really matters* will think any less of him."

Kaitlyn looks as if I've slapped her across the face. "Do you want to know *why* this is my business? Ev and I were a couple!"

If she was aiming to shock any of us, she'll be disappointed. I kind of leaked that information to Margot and Deana already. "I know. He told me."

"We're not blood-related." Kaitlyn's speaking off screen, probably to Margot and Deana, who must be giving her some of their most judgmental looks. I've been on the receiving end of *those* from Deana quite a bit this past year. But Kaitlyn's not too shabby there, either—even in profile. I'm surprised I don't hear them collapsing to the floor beneath her scorching eyes of rage.

"Yeah, well," Kaitlyn picks up her tirade against me, "I bet he didn't tell you that we're *soulmates*. That it doesn't matter how many other people we date, it doesn't matter if we're separated, I am him and he is me."

Wow. Talk about being too obsessed with *Wuthering Heights*. I cock my head. "I don't get that impression from him. Especially since you got married to someone else rather than risk losing *your* trust fund."

Kaitlyn's eyes are glistening. "I bet he didn't tell you that Addy's *his* daughter, though, did he? Not Blake's?"

My mouth is open, ready to give some retort, but when my brain registers what she's just said, I shut it closed. Kaitlyn smiles, and it's the first time I've seen anything other than anger on her face. It's not a very welcoming smile, though.

"Thought not," she says. "And if he's keeping that from you, what else is he lying to you about?"

I still want to say something—that it's none of her business, that her telling me not to date him is making me want to date him even more just to wipe that grin off her face, but if Addy is their daughter, that's a whole lot of baggage I don't know if I can deal with. Especially right now, at my age. Motherhood isn't exactly on the to-do list before 'figure out what the hell I want to do with my life.'

"Here." The video shakes as Kaitlyn's presumably handing the phone back to Margot or Deana. "And stay away from my café." Nice to know she treats even friends of her enemies with contempt. I'm starting to wonder whether or not she's more Lady Catherine de Bourgh than Catherine Earnshaw.

Margot cringes when she's back in focus. "Sorry about that."

Deana pops her head onto the screen. "We didn't think she'd actually notice us ... "

"Forget about it." I swallow. "Thanks for letting me know."

"June—" Deana looks concerned.

I hear the café bell ring again. "You better go," I say. "I have to get to bed. Good night!" I end the call before they can say anything more.

And I sit there on my bed, my fingers tracing my lips. My blood runs cold, and I've forgotten that feeling. I've forgotten that taste.

That might have been something to tell me before he started making out with me. I stare at the table beside my bed, at the hardcover book I've put there. I can't even look at it without shaking. I pick it up and shove it under my bed, switching the lamp off and burying my head into my pillow.

CHAPTER SEVENTEEN

*S*leeping—or more accurately, tossing and turning until you finally drift off due to exhaustion after the sun's risen—atop your bed spread doesn't make for a very refreshing feeling when your alarm clock goes off what feels like minutes after you've finally lost consciousness. But knowing that if you dare to hit 'snooze' even once, your step-dad is going to knock on the door, let himself in before you answer, and see you on top of your blankets in an unprofessional state of disarray works better than coffee to give you just enough energy to roll out of bed and force yourself into the bathroom.

I don't even know how I get from bed to bathroom to clean clothes to Cooper's car, but I do. My body goes through the motions even if my mind is stuck on another planet.

Every time I try to think about books or something else to soothe me, Rockford's face replaces one of the main characters and I picture myself at the heroine's lowest point. Elizabeth seeing Pemberley and starting to regret turning down Darcy's proposal. Jane banishing herself to the moors and then living with the Rivers, determined to put all thoughts of love behind her.

Catherine on her death bed, still making her life more dramatic and painful than it needed to be.

"You seem out of sorts this morning, Junie."

I don't know what's worse: working at Cooper's office or riding with my parents in their carpool almost every day. Or just with Mom when he has to stay late. Not that he hasn't tried to get me to stay late with him to "get a start on tomorrow." Like all the filing and data entry I do can't possibly be done within an eight-hour work day. Sometimes I'm done so early, I have to ask for additional projects. Which is how I spent yesterday morning shredding page after page of decades-old documents.

"I'm fine," I say, after who knows how long. My voice cracks as I open my mouth.

Cooper sighs as we pull up to a stoplight, and he rests his elbows on the steering wheel.

"Your father's just worried about you, honey," says Mom. Again with 'your father.'

I'm not in much of a charitable mood. "My *step*-father."

Cooper smacks his lips as he makes a turn. "You know, June, it wasn't easy pulling strings to get you this job so late into the summer season, so if you're having regrets about giving up your library thing—"

"I still think you could volunteer for the library *and* work during the day, if you really want—"

"Morgan, she's distracted enough." Cooper speaks into the mirror now, and I wish he'd just focus on the road. "She's already got an in with the Rockfords since they're inviting her to babysit. She can socialize with them outside of her responsibilities—"

"I'm done with the library," I say, interrupting their pseudo-argument about what I should or shouldn't do like they get to make all the decisions for me. That shuts them both up immediately.

Cooper's positively beaming as we pull up to Mom's workplace to drop her off. "Good. That's good, Junie. Shows you're developing a good head on your shoulders."

I stare at the phone in my hand as Mom and Cooper twist and turn across the car seats to share a peck. I don't know *why* I'm holding the phone, staring at a message I got from Rockford this morning: *Thank you so much for your help last night! And for... everything else. I want to see you soon.*

I'm more confident than ever that I've made the right decision to leave the library behind.

I don't want to see you anymore, I type. *Sorry.*

"Well," says Cooper, looking over his shoulder as he pulls out of the parking lot. "Another day, another dollar!"

I slide the phone into my pocket, determined not to check it again.

———

BETWEEN SHREDDING AND DATA ENTRY, phone calls and Cooper's too-cheerful blabbering in the mornings, the rest of the week passes into dreary numbness. I couldn't tell you what I did if my life depended on it. Other than shutting my phone off entirely, and emailing Margot and Deana to tell them I was too busy to respond to any messages they might send me. Not that they'd be fooled by my sudden silence.

Tired of me moping around the house yesterday without even explaining why, Mom wouldn't let me have a full weekend's peace. It's Sunday, only four days since practically hooking up to breaking up in a matter of hours. But it feels like four years.

I don't know what Owen did to deserve this punishment, but he isn't allowed to spend Sunday doing nothing, either. But at least in his case, he was playing games instead of staring at the walls. Mom sent Owen and me out to run errands—which translates to me driving all over town with my brother whining about how pointless and dumb him tagging along is and pleading for me to please drop him off at a friend's. He actually proved more of a hindrance than a help while shopping, but at least I roped him into loading the grocery bags into the car. Now we're at Subway, eating sandwiches on Mom's dime at one of the outdoor tables, and his whining has finally died down into a blissful silence.

"So… What happened with you and SJ?"

So much for blissful. My thoughts are so centered on my conversation with Kaitlyn and my brief bit of happiness with Rockford that I've almost forgotten about the sort of confession from Sinjin, even if it happened more recently than my sort of confession from Rockford. But there was that whole mess of revelations that came after that, so you can't really blame me.

"Is something wrong with Sinjin?" It's a stupid question. But I haven't given much thought to the way we parted. I didn't think he could have strong enough feelings for me to feel more than a brief bit of disappointment.

Owen shrugs and takes a massive bite of his pulled pork sub. "He's just down is all. And everyone knows he wanted to ask you out soon."

"He did?" I put down my veggie sub, suddenly losing my appetite. Owen eating such a disgusting sandwich and chewing while talking isn't helping.

"Uh oh." Owen wipes his mouth with a napkin and then takes a sip of his soda. "Did I blow his secret?"

"No." I wrap half of my sandwich back in its paper to keep the food out of sight. "He did sort of confess to me the other day, but—"

"You're dating some other guy, I heard."

I stare at Owen. I'm wondering how many other rumors about my life have circled through the high school track and field team. "I'm not dating anyone." I feel a little bile rise up into my throat and I grab a sip of iced tea to wash the disgusting feeling away.

Owen's jaw drops. "Then why did you say no to SJ?"

I feel suddenly as if I'm on trial, and all the world is staring at me, instead of just my pork-sub-eating brother. I tuck a strand of hair behind my ear and stare intently at the table. "He's a little young for me, Owen."

"You didn't think that a couple of years ago."

"I was in high school then, too. It was different." I hope I'm not blushing. I can feel the heat on my face, but I pray I'm not blushing. But what the hell, I don't question Owen about his love life. I have no idea if he's even ever dated anyone outside of dances.

Owen sighs and takes another large bite. "That's what I told him." He pauses to take a drink. "He's had a rough year."

"Oh? Sorry to hear."

Owen nods. "He wanted to do this study abroad thing, but his parents told him to wait until he was in college. He wasn't even allowed to go with his sisters on their European trip this summer."

"That sucks." But I can see their point. Sure, some high schoolers spend their junior year abroad, but there are plenty of opportunities for that when you're older. *Cling to your teenage innocence while you can. Things get worse later.* I feel like an old lady for thinking it.

"He dated a couple of girls, but it didn't go well." Owen seems like he's telling the story to his sandwich rather than to me. "And he started just … feeling nostalgic, I guess. For his dates with you. For his sisters being home."

"I'm sure *you* missed me, too." I lay on the sarcasm. I can't picture Owen being depressed over not having to deal with his sister.

Owen shrugs and finally finishes his sub off. "You help deflect some of the Mom and Cooper scrutiny, so yeah, sure." He dabs his mouth with his napkin and then grins at me. "So I guess Sinjin and I concocted this plan to get the two of you back together this summer. Something fun for him to look forward to."

"Really. *You* wanted me to date your best friend again."

Owen grins sheepishly. "Okay, it was more *his* idea than mine."

I cradle my cup in my hand and pause before taking a sip. "Did Margot have something to do with this, too?"

Owen laughs. "She might have. Why else do you think she signed up for the volunteer position only to have a sudden change of plans? She knew she wouldn't be here this summer."

I take a drink and shake my head. "You guys should have just been more direct about things."

Owen slides his arms onto the table. "And then you'd have totally missed out on the chance to meet your actual boyfriend, so you should be thanking me."

"He's not my boyfriend." I slam the cup back on the table and rifle through my purse, looking for a Kleenex. My hand grips my phone, which I must have turned on at some point today. Probably out of habit before I left the house, in case Mom forgot something on the grocery list.

Owen smirks. "And that's so not his text you're checking right now."

There are dozens of missed calls and messages. I know most of them have to be from Rockford. I haven't responded for a few days now. I feel like such a coward, keeping my nose to the ground and hoping it'll all go away without me even doing anything about it.

It's like I think I'm a novel heroine, who can mope and lament her lover's betrayal.

Maybe he deserves more from me than that.

"Well." I can hear Owen slurping his cup even though he's clearly run out of soda. "At least you had the guts to tell him no. Gently, I hope." I look up to see Owen staring at his own phone, which he's pulled out from his pocket. He's not talking about Rockford, of course, but Sinjin. "Now he can move on, at least."

I swallow and stare at the text: *Please. We need to talk. Come by my condo this afternoon.*

I shove the phone into my pocket and stand, gathering my garbage. "Let's get these groceries home." I pause, chewing the inside of my cheek. "I have somewhere to be."

CHAPTER EIGHTEEN

My finger floats over the doorbell for far too long, and my brain is running through my list of options, all of them ending in the same thing: Run. Pretend you were never here. Just let it all go away.

No. You owe him this. You'll feel better. You can't just pretend things didn't happen.

I ring the bell.

The few seconds it takes for him to answer feel like much longer. I adjust my purse strap and consider giving myself an A for effort and calling it a day. But the door does open. And Rockford is standing there, his brows furrowed, thick lines of tension twisting his face.

"June!" The lines dissipate, and his expression softens. "Thank god. You came!"

I try peering around him to see if I've walked into one of those impromptu dinner parties, but I don't see anyone. Not that that means they can't be hidden away.

"Come in." Rockford gestures inside.

I chew my lip. "I can't stay long."

I feel Rockford stiffen as I walk past him. I suppose I've made myself clear with those words. But that doesn't mean I get out of giving him a proper rejection.

Rockford closes the door behind me and tells me I can put my purse down on the table. I feel like I should clutch it and stand there and not take a step farther in. *Say what you came to say and get out. The more time you spend here, the farther you step inside, the harder it will be to leave.*

Numbly, I set the purse down, keep my shoes on, and follow Rockford back to that recessed sitting area, around the fireplace, feeling a bit ill as we pass the sunroom. There's no fire going, no other company around the fireplace. There's a glass of water by Rockford's tablet on one of the corner tables.

Rockford gestures awkwardly to the sofa. "Please. Sit down."

I do. And Rockford, instead of sitting kitty-corner from me beside the tablet and water like I expected him to, sits right next to me, leaving only a hand's length of space between us. I shift slightly to put the smallest bit more of extra space there, but I can't go much farther, or I'll be sitting on the table.

"Rock—Mr. Rockford—"

"Everett."

"*Mr. Rockford.*" I take a deep breath and squeeze the edge of the couch cushion. "I'm sorry. I… I'm not looking for a relationship right now."

"You're confused and you're complicated." Rockford nods. "You said as much. June, I… That doesn't matter. You don't need to have your life together to want to invite someone into it."

"I *can't.*" I swallow and pause to get the rhythm of my breathing back to normal. "I'm so sorry I kissed you back that day the beach." I laugh nervously. "That I kissed you a few more dozen times after that. I shouldn't have given you false hope—"

Rockford is studying me, his eyes flitting over my face and looking for something. I can't keep looking back. I focus on the floor, how my shoes sink into the thick, cushiony carpet.

"June, don't lie." I feel Rockford's hand on mine, and I almost convulse. I shudder, slipping the hand gently out of his grip. "I *need* you."

I don't know whether to melt or to run for the hills. My brain is shouting at me—he can't *need* you after barely two months, he doesn't even know you—but my heart is pounding, remembering those moments when Rochester, Heathcliff and Darcy exclaimed much the same to the women they loved.

I cradle the hand he touched in my lap, out of his reach. "This all happened too fast. And I can't. I just can't."

"If you tell yourself you can't, then you won't!" Rockford takes a deep breath and lays a hand on my shoulder. "June, this isn't a matter of some sort of outside obstacle." I guess he hasn't talked to his sister since he told her he was *dating* me. "You're throwing up walls yourself."

"No outside obstacle?" I turn, twisting my shoulder out of his grasp, sighing incredulously. "You don't know anything about me! I don't really know anything about *you!*" *This is ridiculous. Surely Kaitlyn gloated about our phone call. Surely he knows what set this off.*

Rockford grabs both of my shoulders and twists me toward him. He doesn't do so roughly, but I'm taken aback. "I know everything I need to know to know that I love you!"

I'm speechless. I didn't think that was an actual thing that happened to actual people. But I can't even open my mouth. All I can think about is how he didn't pick up on the anvil-sized hint I gave him to bring up the issue of Kaitlyn and Addy and instead focused on not needing to know anything about *me*. Like *I* have something to hide.

… And he thinks he *loves* me.

I can't even. It's way too soon for that. I just can't deal with it. Countless hours spent reading and watching my favorite romance stories, and I just can't *deal* with it in real life. I can't. I use both hands to flick his hands away and he lets them fall. I can't even look him in the face.

"What *happened?*" he asks. "How can your attitude toward me change so much in just a few days? In *one* day? You totally ignored me after Wednesday, except for a text saying you don't want to see me anymore." He lets out a deep breath and runs his hand through the hair atop his forehead. "I thought you…" He runs a hand over his mouth, stopping himself from saying whatever it was he was about to say.

"You thought I what?" I cross my arms, recognizing the bitchy tone I've taken with Deana bubbling to the surface. "That I *loved* you?"

"Yes!" Rockford throws his hands in the air. He turns to me, his expression softening, then tightening again. He swallows. "June, do you know what I risk to be with you? I knew it was stupid to fall in love with you, but I did anyway—"

I scoff. "Well, if *that* isn't a tempting confession, I don't know what is!" I stand, my anger threatening to make my head explode. I pound down the hallway, and I can hear Rockford scrambling to follow after me.

"June, I'm sorry. That came out the wrong way—"

I spin around, jabbing a finger at his chest, doing my best to seem menacing even if I have to stare upward to look at him. "It doesn't matter how it *came out*, it's the truth. I've known from the start you didn't like me—"

"Didn't like you? I just told you I *loved* you—"

I take a step backward. "You don't know what love *is*. Not if you think you're in love with someone you find just *bearable*."

"What the hell are you talking about?"

We've reached the entryway and the kitchen counter now, and I'm grabbing for my purse, rifling through for my keys. Rockford slips in beside me, clamping down on the bag so I have no choice but to glare at him.

"I *heard* you tell Blake I was 'bearable.' Not someone you'd want to go out with."

Rockford's eyes search my face. "I don't know what you're—"

I practically stomp my foot. "In the *clothes store*." I shake my head. "Never mind, that's not even important—"

Some sort of dawning washes over Rockford's face. His grip on the purse weakens and I rip it out from his grip. "You heard that? No, I—I mean, it was a stupid thing to say. I was just embarrassed, and dating someone I'd just met—someone who'd knocked me over in the rainstorm—was nearly the last thing on my mind. But even then, I was sort of into you—"

I slide the purse strap over my shoulder and fish out the keys. "I'm sure." I flail my hands out in response to Rockford's unrelenting stare. "Because dating a 'most generous' Rockford who hasn't enough courtesy or understanding of how to interact with people outside of his little clique was definitely *not at all* on mine."

Rockford's shoulders stiffen, and his head tips upward so that he's looking down on me—almost haughtily. "So *that*'s what you think of me? That I'm some snobbish rich asshole who wasn't *at all* risking his entire inheritance to date someone his mother didn't pick out for him—"

I shrug my shoulders and cross my arms defiantly. "I didn't ask you to. And that's beside the point." The door bell rings, and the tension drops out of Rockford's face as his eyes flick to the door behind me, his mouth twisting into a frown. We're in a standoff, saying nothing, the only sound the incessant ringing of the bell. And then several knocks. And more and more bell ringing.

"*Stop that.*" I can just barely make out the voice from the other side of the door.

"Uncle Ev!"

"Isla, can you quit bossing her around?"

"I will if she gets on Ritalin or something so I can have some peace and quiet."

"You better get that," I say, having no interest in being here when the woman his mother wants him to marry barges in with his possible daughter and the poor man once married—still married but separated? I can't even keep up with the details—to his sister/lover. "I'm done with all of this drama."

I tiptoe nearer to Rockford and lower my voice in case anyone on the other side of the door can hear me. Not likely under the pounding and the doorbell. "What do I care if you were risking your inheritance for me? You weren't doing that *for me*. Not *really*." I sigh and point to the door. "Maybe you just wanted to escape all of that."

"Oh, come *off* it, Blake!" shouts Isla. "She doesn't know what Ritalin *is*!"

"That doesn't—" starts Blake, but he seems suddenly interrupted. "Captain! Come back! Here, boy!"

I readjust the strap on my purse and lean back, standing straighter. "But I'm not some romantic heroine you can just use to escape reality. I'm not some end goal." I unlock the door and grip the handle. I lower my eyes and toss one more comment over my shoulder. "I want to be with someone who knows where he's going. And I want to know that wherever *I'm* going, we'll make a great pair. And that entails complete honesty. If you want fantasy, hook back up with Kaitlyn. You seem devoted to your idea of her anyway." I pull open the door and come face to face with Blake and Isla—Blake surprised, and Isla almost equally so, but I see she has room to look down at me from over the top of her nose—just as Addy buries her head into my abdomen.

"June!" she screams, just as I hear Rockford call, "June!" behind me.

His voice rings out louder, desperate, even panicked. But I spare a smile for Blake and pat Addy's back. "Nice to see you, Addy." I pull her gently apart just as Captain comes bolting across the lawn and settles into Addy's embrace. I nod at the very blonde siblings. "Blake. Isla."

"June, how have you—"

"My, I haven't seen *you* since—"

But I don't hear the rest of what they have to say. I'm down the sidewalk, smiling at Addy as she and Captain tumble on the small front lawn, tuning out Isla's shrieks of how Addy is dirtying her new outfit, and head down the sidewalk to my car.

I unlock the door and sit down in front of the wheel, all confidence, all bluster. I toss the purse on the passenger seat and take out my phone, ready to bombard Margot and Deana out of the blue with the details of the scene I've just lived—and how it reminds me of the argument Elizabeth and Darcy have after his first proposal. Even if the situation was almost completely different.

What are you saying? They're not even remotely the same. Look around you. Not exactly Regency England, is it?

I'm not in the mood to have them tease me that it all wound up working out with Elizabeth and Darcy in the end. I'm not in the mood to explain any of this, to keep reliving these books like I'm in some sort of wild fantasy. It obviously doesn't work out for me like it does for Jane or Elizabeth. Maybe it's about time I thank my lucky stars I don't die of despair like Catherine and get back to reality.

Sorry I've been busy, I text. *And sorry we've spent so much time talking about me. You guys are in FRANCE. Tell me more about what you've been up to.*

I toss the phone down on top of the passenger seat, start the car, put it in reverse and grip the steering wheel, ready to lose myself in reality.

CHAPTER NINETEEN

$\mathcal{A}$ year ago, Deana and I might have been walking down Michigan Avenue, doing more window-shopping than shopping-shopping on our I-know-it's-a-stereotype-but-it's-true ramen-noodle budgets. Of course, a part of me is fully aware that I'm romanticizing last year by thinking of the fun first month we had together as college freshmen, conveniently pushing aside the rest of the year and how we may as well have been strangers sharing a room.

I don't care. There's a lot to be said of romanticizing the past, if it'll help you escape a dreary present.

Blame a few months of working in Cooper's office for draining just about all of the bluster out of me.

At least I'm romanticizing my real life now. Instead of seeing fictional men where there are none.

I try to think of the stores Deana and I visited together a year before, but I draw a blank. There are endless clothes stores, so I can't remember where we tried on Homecoming dresses laughing our asses off that we weren't even going to a Homecoming. I can't remember which of the endless cell phone stores had the cute cell phone guy Deana instantly fell in love with for the rest of the day.

All I remember is he had "biceps I couldn't even wrap both hands around," as Deana kept saying, and how she held out her hands in a circle as if to give meaning to the picture.

I had all of one month in which I was completely and utterly in love with college life before it all blended into misery.

I stop at the end of the block to wipe my nose with one of the Kleenexes from my purse and toss it into the garbage bin, telling myself my nose always does that when I walk outdoors for long periods, and it's not because I'm fighting off tears so hard I can feel the pressure building up in my forehead. I take a deep breath and look around, not sure of the nearest L stop. I'm not entirely familiar with the cross street I've decided to stop at. Fine. It's not like I want to get back to my dorm room and the roommate I've seen for all of three minutes while we were both awake. I decide to walk down the street, see where my feet take me.

They don't take me very far when I notice a used bookstore. *Why not? Maybe you can find some new classics. Hopefully ones that don't involve romance or putting jerks and liars on pedestals.*

I go in and start browsing the nearest tables. A shopkeeper steps up after a minute and asks if I need help, but I politely send her on her way. I'm looking through the aisles, one after the other, not knowing what it is I'm looking for. Almost thinking it's possible that some book about gardening or the Civil War or politics is going to jump off the shelf and tell me where I'm supposed to be going, give me an anchor that will keep my feet on the ground.

My fingers rest on a copy of *Jane Eyre*, misfiled under the non-fiction section. I pull it off the shelf and open it, my fingers shaking as I see I'm at the part where Jane hears her name on the moors.

If this was my life, I think, I'd hear Rockford calling for me. I'd be headed back to him, battered and broken and free from the things that bound him to another life.

He'd also have kept a secret wife locked away in his attic, June. Get over it already. Your life isn't some romantic fantasy novel from another era. It's this. This life where love doesn't work out, where things aren't tied up with a nice little bow, where the most you can hope for is you find something you can stand to do in the hours between waking up and going to bed.

"*June!*" I *do* hear it. The way he said my name as I walked away. I can still hear it ringing in my ears.

I try to put the book back with trembling fingers, and I suddenly start making sense of the murmurs I've been hearing, the voice over a speaker coming from a microphone.

"… thank you for coming all the way out here on what's an alarmingly bitter day for September. But I guess you have to expect some wind in the windy city."

I catch a glimpse of some of the group gathered at the back corner of the shop as they laugh at the host's poor attempt at humor.

"I'm looking around and I see a dozen phones. I know a few of you had tablets out before I started talking—some of you still do." There are a few guilty chuckles. "How many of you just hand your kids one of these when you're out and about and tired and the kids are getting whiny and you're just like 'shut up, I've had a bad day'?"

I see a few people raise their hands, and I move closer, cheesy host or no. I'm genuinely curious for reasons I don't even comprehend.

"With so much to compete for young children's attention these days, it's harder and harder to remind parents that a child's love for reading starts when they're young. That it's the parents' job to seek out activities that promote a love for literature."

I step out from the end of the aisle and slip in behind the crowd. There's an empty seat a row over.

"With that in mind, I invited a speaker here today who made time for children's literacy efforts even while helping to run a miniature empire in his small community. Please join me in welcoming Everett Rockford."

The small crowd starts clapping. I'm hovering over the empty seat as Rockford gets out of his up by the microphone. I'm frozen, unable to sink into the crowd in time. He gets up to the microphone, his tablet in hand. He looks as if he's been up all night—for days even—to prepare for this speech. He's got dark circles under his eyes, and his lips are hardened into a thin line. He places the tablet on the podium and looks up for the first time. He's smiling —or trying to. His eyes scan the room.

"Thank you. I'm—" He stops. His eyes have met mine. Because I've been too stupid to sit down or run. Although running probably would have called attention to myself, too.

Still, it's either that or disturb his presentation when I have no business being here.

I slip back the way I came and head down one of the aisles. It takes an incredibly long time to get down the aisle. I can still hear speaking over the microphone. "… Mr. Rockford?"

"Oh. Yes. Sorry. Um. Will you excuse me?"

I am so busted.

"Mr. Rockford?"

I turn the corner and am out the door. *Run, run. Get away. Get down the street and he won't find you.*

I stop suddenly. I'm standing outside the bookstore and I'm still holding that copy of *Jane Eyre*. Cursing, I open the door and head back in. I toss the book on the nearest table, not caring, and clutch the door handle.

"June!"

A hand touches my shoulder, and I melt. I turn around. He's breathless, a flush of red to his cheeks.

"I'm sorry," I say, looking down. For what? For how I chickened out when he offered me the chance at something more over the summer? For how I can't get over him even now? "I didn't know you were a speaker here. I swear. I just walked in—"

The door opens and I jump, my hand slipping from the handle. Rockford grabs my arm and leads me gently aside, deeper into the bookstore, to make room for the people entering. "I don't care." His lips curl into that sad, lilted smile I've seen too many times. "In fact, I believe you. If you'd known I was here, you never would have gone in, would you?"

"You should go back." I chew the inside of my cheek. "I can't believe you just walked out in the middle of a presentation."

"It's fine. I'll explain later. But June, I can't let you go. Can't you see? It's like something guided you to me."

I say nothing. I notice his hand's gentle pressure on my arm hasn't lessened, but I don't struggle to make him let go.

"I knew you went back to school in Chicago." He lets his hand fall, and I have to stop myself from telling him not to let go. "I asked Deana when I found out she was your friend. But I knew I couldn't just show up at your dorm room door."

The very idea is too much for my brain to handle. "How's Deana doing at the library?" Because if I ask civil enough, I just might be able to get this conversation back to awkward-acquaintance level.

"Great. Violet likes her." Rockford sighs. "It's painful to be there, though, June. The story time room—"

"—and Kaitlyn."

"No. *You.*" Rockford's eyes search mine, and I can't keep staring. I have to look away.

"Well, at least story time is over for the year." I clear my throat. "You don't have an excuse to go there so often."

Rockford laughs. "When's the last time you talked to Deana?"

I'm not expecting that question at all. I raise an eyebrow. "Last week, I guess. I've been busy." *Ignoring her texts. Because ignoring her worked out so well last time.*

"I work at the library now. Full-time." He chuckles. "Violet had to create a children's literature position for me, but I helped her figure out she had plenty of room in their budget after years of relying on donations. And I'm going back to school to get my library science degree."

He may as well have just told me he worked on the moon and is studying robotics. "What?"

Rockford smiles. "I told Mother—well, Kathleen—I wasn't

going to marry Isla or anyone else she suggested. That I was done with the whole Rockford enterprise."

"Why?" My lips pinch. "Is it because she heard about you and Addy?"

Rockford shakes his head. "No. June, I don't know what you thought about that. If that's what you meant when you thought I was still devoted to Kaitlyn—"

"No. It wasn't that." How do I explain he seemed more in love with the idea of being in love than the idea of being in love with *me*? That the crazy romance he had with Kaitlyn as a teen was something straight out of a romance novel, something I stupidly wanted for years, something I was too afraid to actually experience given the chance. I switch gears. "I heard you might be Addy's real father!" I notice the clerk who asked me if I needed help glance up from behind the checkout counter. I lower my voice. "From Kaitlyn herself."

"That's a lie." Rockford shakes his head. "And that woman has no right to say anything about Addy, no matter what happened between her and Blake. She left her to Blake and—" He pauses. "Forget about it. But is that why you wanted nothing to do with me? You were afraid Addy was secretly my daughter?"

I run a hand over my arm. "That was part of it." I look up and meet his eyes. "Rockford, you don't understand. I've been living like a zombie. I keep jumping into my favorite books like they're some sort of way to block the pain of the life I've chosen to live." I scoff at myself. "You crossed the line from fantasy to reality that day you told me you loved me. It was like my romantic fantasies coming to life. I couldn't deal with it. I can't deal with anything."

Rockford places both hands on my arms, rubbing them softly. "June, you're too hard on yourself." He cocks an eyebrow. "And please, call me Everett. Or Ev."

"Oh!" I place a hand over my mouth. I didn't even realize I'd said what I call him in my head out loud. "I'm sorry."

"It's okay." He spots something down one of the aisles of books and reaches for my hand. I let him guide me down the aisle to a quiet corner with a couch and a coffee table. "Were you afraid that I was caught up in an ideal, too? Like I was when I dated Kaitlyn?"

I nod, too afraid to look at him.

He sighs. "Maybe you were right. Maybe I didn't even know it myself at the time, but in all these months since then—I've done a lot of thinking. I've done more than just think. I've decided where I'm going. So I can prove I'm ready to let someone else into my life, so I can let her know I choose a life *with* her, not a life comprised *of* her."

He squeezes my hand and I look up at him and smile.

"You know, standing up to my mother was one of the hardest things I've ever done." Rockford—Everett—sits on the couch and tugs on my arm, patting the couch and gesturing for me to sit next to him. "And I wasn't the only one to face the consequences." He squeezes my hand. "When she found out I'd gone to work at the library, she completely pulled all the Rockford funding."

"I'm surprised Violet didn't fire you on the spot."

Everett laughs. "Maybe part of her considered it. But she's a good woman. She knows it was me who really kept improving the library. And it's already got all the money invested in construction and improvements. It's not like Mother can get it back."

"Does that apply to your condo, too?" I think achingly of the one good evening we spent there.

Everett's grin reaches his eyes, and his irises light up in a way I haven't seen in a while. "You might hope so, but until the trust fund was supposed to kick in, the place was in Mother's name." He shakes his head. "It doesn't matter. Blake and Addy let me move in with them."

"And Captain." I try to smile, but my lips are trembling.

"And Captain." Everett rubs a thumb over the back of my hand. "You know, it was because that dumb dog got away from me that day that I almost plowed into you."

"You mean when I 'got in your way'?"

Everett tsks. "You really didn't have a favorable impression of me in those early days, did you?"

"I hardly had time to change my mind before you were confessing your love."

"But you *did* change your mind."

"I..." I look down at the coffee table, taken aback by the three books I find sitting there: *Jane Eyre*, *Pride and Prejudice* and *Wuthering Heights*. I slip my hand from Everett's and trace my fingers across the nearest cover.

"That was me." Everett picks up *Wuthering Heights*, and I can't help but think of the hardcover book I couldn't bring myself to throw away. Last I knew it was still there, under my bed at home, out of sight, but often on my mind. "I had some time to kill when I got here this morning. In case you're wondering if it was some cosmic sign."

"What?" I find myself laughing without even knowing why.

"Deana told me..." He clears his throat. "That you kept comparing me to the romantic heroes in these three books over the summer."

I half-heartedly punch his shoulder. "She did *not!*" Seriously. Why was she talking about me to him?

"She did." Everett's smile transforms his rigid face with his too-pointy nose into something beautiful, something stunning. "If she hadn't convinced me you might have been even a fraction as in love with me as I am with you, I don't think I could have bounced back this week like I have."

'As I am,*' he says.* I'm blushing. "'Bounced back'?"

Everett tosses the book back on the table and leans forward, wrapping me in his arms. I freeze, not knowing what to do. *If you hug him back, you'll just be more confused.* I wrap my arms around his back and nestle my face into his chest. *No. When you hug him back, for the briefest of moments, for the shortest of seconds, you're more sure of yourself than you ever are.*

"June, I don't know if you want me to be like these men —"

"I don't."

He laughs, and I feel the beat of his heart through my ear against his chest. "Good. I was going to say, they're all fairly awful to different degrees. Although I can see why you lumped me in with them."

He pulls away, and I clutch harder. He stops and there's just enough room between us so we can look at each other's faces. "I don't think you're like them at all," I say. And it's the truth.

Everett cocks his head. "My life has been pretty dramatic. And I've been pretty sour because of it."

I bury my head back into his chest. "Better than becoming numb to life's drama."

"If you say so." Everett squeezes me. "I'm sorry I was ever a jerk to you. I am. I'm enjoying life so much more now that it's simpler. Now that I'm doing something I really want to do." He lifts one hand from my back and rubs the back of my head. "I just wish you could feel that way, too."

I pull back and look at him. "My life is simple. And drama-free. Opening myself up to a relationship complicates that."

His face falls. I feel like a monster, like I've stabbed him and twisted the knife. I smile and take his face in my hand. "But I guess I'm just going to have to comes to terms with life being complicated."

The panic washes clear of his features and he bends into my hand, leaning forward and locking his lips with mine. I close my eyes and feel his kiss wash away the panic, the numbness, the uncertainty. It's a better escape than my favorite books. And it's real. It's right here in my hands.

After what seems like both forever and not long enough, I pull away. "Everett, I'm not happy." I drop my hand from his face and grab his hand in mine. "Will you help me? I can't... I can't do this alone."

Everett touches his forehead to mine. "You can. But you won't have to."

EPILOGUE

*I*t's raining when I pull Deana's car up to the library. A sane person would just leave the car running and wait for her best friend to come running out to get in. But no sane person could be as in love as I am.

I park the car and dive out into the rain, no umbrella, no rain coat. I run through the gushing water, my heart fluttering as I pass the drop-off bin—no one's insane enough to be collecting books in this downpour—and seek shelter under the overhang. I shake my hands out and wring some of the moisture from my hair, and then I head inside, fully aware I'm dripping water all over the entryway.

"June! Sheesh, what are you doing?" Deana appears in the entryway from inside the library, her umbrella halfway open. "I would have run out to meet you."

I grin.

She shakes her head and rolls her eyes. "He's putting books away in the story time room." I toss her the keys and she catches them, clumsily. "If you're not in the car in two minutes, I'm going to class without you!"

I *should* be worried. I probably can't afford to miss a class since

I transferred in a few weeks late. True, it's "just community college," and it "won't get me any good jobs," according to Cooper, but since I'm living with Deana and not 'burdening' my parents at home, it doesn't really matter what he thinks anymore.

And at least Mom still has me over for dinner once a week. With Everett in tow. Cooper can't make a fuss when he thinks a Rockford is dining at his table. (Well, one is. But not a Rockford with much power to get me—or Cooper—a six-figure job.)

"June!" Gracia whisper-shouts my name as I pass by the information desk and I wave, trying to rush past before Violet appears and has a fit about the water I'm dragging onto the carpet.

I slip into the story time room and see Everett on the iron-wrought chair in the back corner. A small group of children are seated on the pillows, some moms and a dad beside them. It's not an official story time, but I know my boyfriend can't resist holding an impromptu one when asked.

"… And that's why the goat ate everything in sight." Everett's positively beaming as he reads the story to the kids, closing the picture book shut. He looks up and his eyes meet mine. I didn't think it was possible that he could look any happier, but he does.

Addy jumps up from the cushions and grabs the book from Everett. "Can I see?"

She already has it in her hands and is walking over to the small kids table. "Addy, please wait for your uncle to answer before you grab it. And please say 'please.'" Blake is up trailing after Addy, but she's not paying attention to him at all. "Hi, June!" he says cheerfully, and before I can reply, he's at the kids table trying to get Addy's attention. Well, I can see where she learned not to wait for a reply.

"What are you doing here?" I'm so distracted by the kids and parents dispersing that I jump when I feel the arm slipping around my shoulder. "You're soaking!"

I look up and grin before wrapping my arms around him and squishing myself hard against his chest. "And now you are too!" I pull away and lean up on my toes, inviting him for a kiss. "I was picking up Deana."

Everett kisses me once, quickly, and not satisfied, kisses me two more times. "She didn't tell me you were stopping by."

"I'm supposed to be in the car on my way to class by now."

"Damn." Everett pulls me tight against him again. "Think she'll notice if I kidnap you?"

"Yeah. But she might not care. I have less than a minute before she's taking off without me."

Everett runs a hand through the hair at the back of his head. "Sheesh. Talk about deadline-oriented. You'd think she was the budding journalist and not the one going for her library science degree."

Yeah, I settled on journalism. I have no idea if it's right for me, but so far, I'm loving the classes in the degree. And not that it should matter, but I could tell Mom was pleased I'd picked something myself. Even Cooper didn't argue that journalism was a dying career field, although I'd prepared my arguments for such an assault. He just made sure to remind me that the future was the Internet and TV, not print. Because someone a couple of decades younger *so* wouldn't already know that.

I considered enrolling in Deana's librarian program. But all that 'practical career' drilling might have been entrenched too deep. "Come on, you know you find it thrilling, the idea of me in a trench coat, tracking down the latest breaking news." I picture Kermit the frog as a reporter and laugh, hugging him harder. "Besides, there might be enough librarians in the family." I blush at what I've said. Not really, 'the family.' Not yet.

"Hmm. I like the sound of that." He leans in for another kiss and comes up for air after a few seconds. "But we'll take it slow, June. Don't worry. You're not shackled to me yet."

"Ew!" says one of the kids. I guess I forgot we're surrounded by children looking through bins of picture books. And parents, too. I let my eyes dart across the room to the grown-ups staring, one mom quickly shuffling her kid out of the room.

"No, but I'm tied to you." I turn my attention back to the moors, to the beautiful countryside house that exists on the walls and in our imaginations. I hold up my pinky finger. "And it'll hurt me as much as it hurts you if that string ever breaks."

He stares at me for a long time, although it probably feels longer than it really is. I watch his eyes roll over my face, taking in everything about me, reaching deep inside trying to see my heart. He cups my face in his hands and kisses me, far longer than before, for what feels like forever.

"June! Seriously? Let's go!"

We break apart and I imagine the sheepish smile on my face looks somewhat like the one on Everett's. "Guess she didn't leave without me."

Everett slaps my back lightly. "Go get 'em, tiger!"

"Are we living a comic book now?" Briefly, I see visions of my life climbing up walls by night, taking photographs—or writing headlines—by day. Didn't I think I had a Spidey sense this summer?

"No," says Everett. He crosses his arms. "We're living *our* life. The rest is just fun. Why would we want to escape?"

"Our *life*," huh? I'm surprised to find that 'I could get used to that' isn't even the first line that pops into my head. Because I already am. *Jane, Elizabeth, Catherine, and now Everett... Thank you for keeping me sane.*

A Love for the Mistletoe

A Love for the Pages Prequel Short Story

JOY PENNY

A LOVE FOR THE MISTLETOE (PREQUEL SHORT STORY)

Set two and a half years before that fateful summer June Eyermann spent at the library, *A Love for the Mistletoe* is a prequel short story about how June and Sinjin started "sort of" going out in high school.

June, a junior in high school, decides to attend her school's Holiday Dance stag. She figures at the very least, she'll have her favorite books to occupy her. Little does she know that the school's photography club's "Kissing Beneath the Mistletoe" event will make this a dance she'll never forget.

"Now, *that's* just cheesy." Deana examined the sparkly green shade she'd painted her nails, but I knew that wasn't what she found so ridiculous.

I put my own sparkly-red-tipped nails on my lap and looked across the room at the backup of people Deana was referring to. To get into the gym-turned-fake-winter-wonderland, you had to pass under mistletoe. Even with the teacher chaperones parked a few feet away at the punch-and-Christmas-cookies table, couples had no qualms about kissing each other in front of a photography club member snapping pics just because a couple of sprigs of fake leaves and berries were dangling overhead. I blushed at the idea of kissing someone so publicly. I blushed at the idea of the guy who popped into my head when I thought of doing just that.

Deana gave up examining her nails and leaned back on the bleacher. "Joe didn't have the money for the donation for a picture, but he still tried to kiss me when we passed under it. I was having none of that. I thought he was such a gentleman." She wrinkled her nose in disgust. "As if. He's more like a perverted abominable snowman." Joe, decked out in an entirely white suit, had left his date several dances ago to go talk with his friends over by one of the basketball hoops. He lifted both hands and growled, as if on cue, causing one of the girls nearby to shriek in delight.

I laughed and pulled my shawl tighter over my shoulders. A strapless shiny blue dress might make me look like the perfect ice princess for the Holiday Dance, but it was in the single digits outside and the gym wasn't exactly doing the best job at keeping the indoors that much warmer. I searched the crowd for Deana's twin sister. "Where's Margot?"

Deana shrugged and gestured to the long line of couples lining up for the mistletoe. "Her date actually *asked* permission to kiss her for the camera, so she took him up on it."

I shook my head as I spotted her in line. "The tragedy." I grabbed the clutch purse I kept next to my waist and grinned, thinking of Margot's smiling face. *She* certainly didn't think it was cheesy.

"What do you keep in there, a book?"

I froze as I pulled the small, tattered paperback out of my clutch purse. I guess I *had* stretched the material to cram it in there.

"Oh. I was joking, but…" Deana leaned over my shoulder. "Oo. *Pride and Prejudice*?"

I felt a rush of excitement. "You're a fan?" I'd only been friends with the twin transfer students for a couple of weeks, if that.

They'd been paired up with me for lab and we'd immediately hit it off. They just didn't see me much outside of class yet, or they'd notice the books I kept within reach at all times, in case a lull in activity ever bored me. Like the lull in activity that was going to a dance without a date.

"Sure. Mamma showed Margot and me the BBC version years ago." She squeezed her hands together. "Colin Firth! I wish he was my date to the dance instead of Joe."

I sniggered. "I don't think the chaperones would approve, considering you're underage and he's like your dad's age. Maybe your grandpa's age."

Deana shrugged. "They'd get over it. His British charm would win them over." She grabbed my book from me and started flipping through it. I almost ripped it out of her hands, but I knew sane people didn't think of their books as their babies. "Can I borrow this?"

"Sure," I said, tucking my hair back behind my ear. "Just… Take good care of it."

Deana rolled her eyes. "I wasn't going to drop it in the punch bowl, if that's what you mean." She stared at the book and gestured for me to go. "Speaking of, could you get us a couple of glasses?"

"I was going to read—"

"Uh uh!" Deana cut me off. "You've been sitting here since you got here. Get up and get *out* there! Why come to a dance if you're just going to read?"

I could ask you the same thing, I thought as I walked away, watching as Deana became engrossed in my novel.

I squeezed through the swaying couples to make my way to the punch table. I grabbed two cups and waited my turn. The couple in front of me was taking an annoyingly long time to select their refreshments, stopping to peck each other every few seconds. The stories I considered the epitome of romance—*Pride and Prejudice* and *Jane Eyre*—didn't have a lot of (or any) kissing. *Wuthering Heights*, well, that was a little different. But casual public displays of affection, it did not have, which was probably a good thing. I was getting pretty uncomfortable watching the couple in front of me.

"Merry Christmas!"

Finally, the couple moved. The girl grabbed the guy's hand, all pretense of taking cookies forgotten.

"Merry Christmas?"

"Oh!" I spun around, not realizing the voice was directed at me. Then I nearly dropped the cups I was holding. "Oh! Oh! Oh!"

I was staring right up into the eyes of my new crush.

"Hi," he said, and his smile was enough to melt even the fake snow all over the gym floor.

"Hi," I said, numbly. "Hi." I winced.

He pointed at the cups in my hand. "Can I help you with those?"

"Uh, sure." I handed him one of the cups and brushed my hair behind my ears nervously. "Thank you."

"No problem." He ladled a scoop of red punch into the plastic cup like a male model on *The Price is Right* with a showcase. "You're one of my sisters' new friends, right?"

"Sisters?" I regretted it the moment I said it. D'uh. Deana and Margot talked about their younger brother. New Indian American guy who transferred in at the same time as them? Obviously said younger brother.

But still. *Younger* brother. When I first saw him in the halls, my heart had skipped a beat. And I could have sworn he was a senior. I mean…. Look at him. He exuded "all grown up."

Or maybe that was just the fact that I kept picturing the two of us locked in an embrace, in what might have been a very "all grown up" setting. I blushed, dying of embarrassment.

He put the cup down and held his hand out for the other. "Deana and Margot?"

"Yeah." I handed him the cup and swallowed. "Yeah. Of course. I mean, yeah." *Hello, tongue? I'd like to be in charge of you again, please.*

He put the second cup down, full of punch, and held out his hand. "I'm Sinjin."

"Hi," I said again, lamely. I scrambled to take his hand in both of mine and shook it rather stupidly. "Hi."

"Uh, what's yours?"

"My…?"

"Your name?"

"Oh! June!"

Sinjin laughed and I dropped his hand like it was a hot potato. He picked up both cups of punch and stepped away from the table to let the people behind us have a turn. I followed him, only to realize he was standing at the edge of the dancing throng, both cups in his hand, not moving.

"Where to?" His eyes scanned the crowd. "Do you have a boyfriend waiting?"

"No boyfriend!" I practically spat the words out. "No boyfriend! No date!" Was it possible to make it any more clearer I had the hots for him? *Dumb, June. Dumb.*

"Oh, cool." Sinjin grinned. "I just saw the two drinks and I assumed…"

"For Deana." I nodded toward the bleachers. Deana was pretty engrossed in my book, even despite the dim light in the gym.

"Oh. Pfft." Sinjin handed me one of the cups and then took a swig from the other. "She can get her own drink."

I laughed and sipped at my punch nervously. I studied him out of the corner of my eye, trying to seem cool and calm, not at all like the mess I felt like inside. I don't know how long we stood there. I seemed to have blocked out all sound but the wild thumping of my heart.

Finish the drink. Then ask him to dance. You can do it. This isn't the 19th or 18th century. A girl can totally ask a guy first.

I took a deep breath and opened my mouth. "Do you—"

"SJ! There you are!"

My handsome Greek god turned his head slightly and I followed his line of sight. Then I cringed. *Oh, god. Owen.*

"Thought we lost you, bud," Owen said, grinning. "Did you find some stag tail like I—ew."

My thoughts exactly. Owen stared at me like I was a smushed cockroach he'd found under his shoe. He looked back at Sinjin. "Dude, this is my *sister.*"

"Oh?" Sinjin studied me, like the thought never occurred to him. "You never mentioned a sister."

I tried to drown myself in the little bit of punch that was left.

"Yeah," said Owen. "Well, you can see why."

"Not really," said Sinjin.

Owen ran a hand through his shaggy blond hair. He looked incredibly underdressed in his polo shirt. Mom had suggested a dress shirt, but Owen was having none of that. Sinjin, on the other hand, looked *incredible* in his dress shirt.

"Well, not only is she my sister, but she's old, you know."

I practically spat my drink back into the cup. "I'm a junior! How is that old?"

Owen thumped Sinjin's chest. "Well, SJ's a freshman like me. You're not one of those gross cougars, are you?"

"Shut up, Owen." I drank the last of the punch and turned on my heel. I felt like dying. As if I wasn't embarrassed enough, Owen had just about assured I could never show my face around Sinjin again. And Sinjin was a *freshman.* What the hell was wrong with me?

I searched for the garbage can, but it was hard to see anything past the people standing at the side of the dance floor. I pushed through a line of them, muttering my excuses, sure I'd seen a can near the door. Sure enough. I dropped the cup in and leaned against the wall, taking a deep breath.

Just forget about it. Forget about him. It's no big deal.

I turned around, about to head back to Deana, and smacked into someone's chest.

"Sorry!"

I took a step back, rubbing my nose, and looked up to see Sinjin. He looked concerned. "You're not bothered by Owen, are you? I haven't been here long, but I know enough about the guy to know he can be a little hard to handle sometimes." He grinned. "Sorry. I know he's your brother. He's cool and all…"

"Don't be." I lowered my hand and clutched my skirt. "As his sister, he makes a point of never showing me his good side."

Sinjin leaned over me, practically hugging me against his shoulder, and dropped his cup into the trash. I inhaled him. He smelled of something rustic, something like pine and spice.

"Do you two want a picture?"

I looked around Sinjin to see the photography club girl with her camera held up. She gestured up with her other hand at the mistletoe.

Oh my god. I just walked over to the mistletoe. With my crush. My eyes searched wildly for the rest of the line, but it'd died down, and there were no others by the mistletoe but us.

"We ask for a $2 donation, but half of it goes to charity," said the girl. "Toys for Tots."

Sinjin showed me a lopsided grin that made my knees wobble. "I can't resist donating to causes benefiting children." He dug his wallet out of his pocket and pulled a couple of bills out. He held the bills out to the girl and looked at me. "I'm not saying we should kiss for the camera. I just thought I'd donate something anyway… I mean, not that I'd be *opposed* to it, I just—"

I stood on my tip toes and planted a kiss on his incredibly soft lips.

The sound of laughter made me come back to the ground. The girl took the dollars from Sinjin's hand. He hadn't moved at all. "Once more, for the camera this time?"

I almost *died*.

"Sure." Sinjin wrapped his hands on my waist. The look of shock was gone, replaced by something like the look you get when curled up in front of the fireplace on Christmas morning. He leaned forward, closing his eyes.

"One, two—" I couldn't hear the girl count "three."

I didn't even notice when she took the picture.

Brielle Reyes may not have post-college life planned out like some of her friends do, but she figures she'll work for her mother's home cleaning service while job hunting for something that makes use of her history and philosophy degrees. It'll work out as long as she doesn't fall in love. Her last relationship was a disaster and she has no idea where she'll be in a few weeks, let alone the rest of her life. Since the only guy in her age range she sees now on a regular basis is cantankerous if handsome client Archer Ward, she probably won't have a hard time sticking to that vow. Probably.

Archer Ward likes very few things: illustrating as a somewhat-celebrated comic artist and his privacy. When his meddling mother hires him a cleaning service on an almost daily basis because she doesn't fully trust her son to live on his own with his disability, he's at first annoyed—even if his house cleaner is the most beautiful woman he's ever spent more than a few minutes with. When he realizes her dreams may take her far outside of his restricted orbit, he has to decide whether to stifle his interest in her or risk messing up her plans to explore if there's something more between them.

Neither can deny they're growing a little fond of each other, even if falling in love just now makes no sense whatsoever. But how often does love ever make perfect sense?

Buy on Amazon - More Purchase Options

Just weeks before graduating, Lilac Townsend throws away her elementary school teacher job offer in Minnesota to work in Florida at the official resort of her favorite vacation spot, Tildy World. Pushing down all second thoughts, she fills her mind with visions of sunny beaches and Tildy Tapir, the cartoon character who always promised to make her childhood dreams come true. Unfortunately, between a sleazy boss and a community college student in a character suit who manages to fray her last nerve, Lilac soon learns that working behind the scenes at the park is hardly "happily ever after."

Nolan Gregosky had plans after graduating high school a few years back: go to college, join a fraternity, and make some memories before earning a degree. Instead, tragedy sidelined those dreams, but his job posing for pictures with drooling, snot-nosed kids as Silly Sandgrouse gives him a chance to unload some pent-up energy. When the stunning but uptight new assistant manager at the resort proves a distraction in more ways than one, Nolan realizes it's up to him to show her what it means to eat, live, and breathe life at the park.

A relationship at this unsteady stage of their lives might not be the brightest idea for either of them, but it's hard to ignore that tingling sensation whenever the paths of this plush-suit beast and naïve beauty collide.

Buy on Amazon - More Purchase Options

All It Takes is one night to change the rest of their lives.

Graduating Uni, travelling Europe and buying her own place – these are on Megan Green's to-do list. At just twenty-two, becoming a mother isn't.

Fast cars, expensive clothes and bedding a different woman every night – this is how Kian Murphy spends his time when not in the MMA ring. Prenatal scans and birthing classes are not on his agenda.

After a chance meeting and passionate encounter, Megan finds herself pregnant with Kian's child. But with a womanizing reputation and a temper that often leads him into trouble, Kian is hardly boyfriend material, let alone father material.

Now Megan and Kian must work out if they have All It Takes to turn their one-night stand into a relationship that will connect them for a lifetime.

All It Takes is a dual-POV new adult, contemporary romance about responsibility, love and discovering who you are in life.

Available on Kindle.

THE TAMING OF THE DUDEBRO

It's summer fun, romance and hilarity in this boxed set containing the first two stories of this series of YA retellings of Shakespeare's classic comedies.

In *The Taming of the Dudebro*, Patricia's dream is coming true: she is directing her own play, a one-act written by her best friend, Grizz, for the school's annual Drama Festival. Everything seems to be perfect until her teacher assigns Kurt Minola, the biggest jerk in the school, to work on her play. Kurt is lazy, selfish and irresponsible. The only good thing about him is his attractive twin brother, Ben—but even he can't seem to change Kurt's attitude. Kurt's presence turns Patricia's dream into a nightmare... until Patricia and Grizz decide to take matters into their own hands, and subject this insufferable surfer-dude to some taming.

Then, in *A Midsummer Night's Dudebro*, with the theater festival behind her and graduation around the corner, Grizz Sheridan figured she was done with Kurt Minola. She wants to focus on spending time with her friends and enjoying her last summer before she goes off to college. No such luck now that Kurt's crushing on her best friend (and his twin brother's girlfriend), Patricia. It seems like he's glued to her side no matter where she goes—class, parties, even Prom. Grizz thinks her luck is changing when she begins working at Merry Mule Coffee Roasters and meets super hottie, Dimitri. That is, until a certain surfer boy starts working there, too—and suddenly seems to have turned his romantic interests elsewhere… Will Grizz survive the summer?

Available now on Kindle.